THE
GREEN
AND
PURPLE
SKIN
OF THE
WORLD

THE GREEN AND PURPLE

stories by
paulo da costa

FREEHAND BOOKS

SKIN OF THE WORLD

© paulo da costa 2013

Canada Council   Conseil des Arts
for the Arts   du Canada

FREEHAND BOOKS GRATEFULLY ACKNOWLEDGES THE SUPPORT OF THE CANADA COUNCIL FOR THE ARTS FOR ITS PUBLISHING PROGRAM. ꝯ FREEHAND BOOKS, AN IMPRINT OF BROADVIEW PRESS INC., ACKNOWLEDGES THE FINANCIAL SUPPORT FOR ITS PUBLISHING PROGRAM PROVIDED BY THE GOVERNMENT OF CANADA THROUGH THE CANADA BOOK FUND.

THIS BOOK IS A WORK OF FICTION. ANY RESEMBLANCE TO ACTUAL PERSONS, LIVING OR DEAD, IS ENTIRELY COINCIDENTAL.

FREEHAND BOOKS
515—815 1ST STREET SW   CALGARY, ALBERTA   T2P 1N3
WWW.FREEHAND-BOOKS.COM

BOOK ORDERS: LITDISTCO
100 ARMSTRONG AVENUE   GEORGETOWN, ONTARIO   L7G 5S4
TELEPHONE: 1-800-591-6250   FAX: 1-800-591-6251
ORDERS@LITDISTCO.CA
WWW.LITDISTCO.CA

LIBRARY AND ARCHIVES CANADA CATALOGUING IN PUBLICATION

DA COSTA, PAULO
THE GREEN AND PURPLE SKIN OF THE WORLD / PAULO DA COSTA.

SHORT STORIES.
ALSO ISSUED IN ELECTRONIC FORMAT.
ISBN 978-1-55481-139-7

I. TITLE.

PS8557.A24474 2013   C813'.6   C2012-907096-3

EDITED BY BARBARA SCOTT
BOOK DESIGN BY NATALIE OLSEN, KISSCUTDESIGN.COM
COVER PHOTO © JLOKIJ / PHOTOCASE.COM
AUTHOR PHOTO BY GALEN BULLARD

PRINTED ON FSC RECYCLED PAPER AND BOUND IN CANADA

To those who suffer and do not know they suffer

"The world shrinks or expands depending on one's courage."

— ANAÏS NIN

FLIES

Foot raised on the shoebox, Senhor Osório sat at the entrance to the tavern enjoying the overdue shine. The question mark of his cane supported his thoughts as he rested his chin on the wrinkled knuckles clasping the wood. His gaze followed the blur of legs striding past.

"Give it a good polish, Armando."

"Yes, Senhor."

Armando stopped, wiped the sweat under his beret and brought his wrinkled hand to his kidney, the gesture intending to readjust it to a tolerable position. The few coins in his vest pocket rattled their protest. Armando hoped there would be plenty of time for leisure in the grave, very soon. He sighed, imagining the day he would at last lie still and someone else would polish his leather.

"They don't make shoes like they used to, Armando. Bought them last Christmas. An import, a treat. Already the seams hang by a thread."

"There's nothing like the olden days, when a shoe was a shoe, that's for sure," Armando agreed, spreading a layer of black paste over the dull shoes.

Senhor Osório's eyes followed the trajectory of a miniskirt to the end of the road. Then to a passing cloud concealing the sunshine. He sighed and lowered his eyes.

"How was she?" asked Armando.

"Divine . . . truly Divine!"

"It's all His fault!"

"Whose fault?" blurted Senhor Osório, startled out of his longing.

"The one up there." Armando half-lifted his hand to the sky, and lacking strength, dropped it. "He seized everything from us, our youth, our looks, but left us the idea, the burning desire."

o

Across the road, Jorge and Tadeu basked in the sun. They lounged, tilting back their iron patio chairs in a measured way, aiming their half-unbuttoned shirts at the golden rays. The undulating heat generated discomfort, a price they accepted for looking perfect. Loud music made prolonged conversation difficult. Their fingernails' tapping on the metal table top accompanied the syncopation of the bass. Jorge and Tadeu, there to see and be seen.

The roar of an expensive motorcycle bettered the noise of the loudspeakers and the boys stirred from the patio, strolled their way to the curb to greet their friend. They exchanged nods and smiles. Tadeu kicked the front tire. The friend clenched his fist around the motorcycle handle and revved it. From a nearby house, a girl ran up the road and mounted the two-wheeled machine. The roar spat a few pebbles in the air and then dissipated in the heat of a summer afternoon.

Jorge and Tadeu glanced at the black figures across the road who shook their disapproving heads.

"Crooked noses run far back in your gene pool, I see!" Jorge said as he slid his sunglasses to the tip of his own nose to better evaluate the grandfathers across the road.

"Yep! Donkey ears in yours!"

"Hah!" chuckled Jorge with a friendly slap on Tadeu's nape.

From the periphery of their vision, and between the spirals of rising cigarette smoke, the boys watched their grandpas. Grandpas with eyes in perpetual rotation, buzzing with curiosity, holding their grandsons in sight. Annoyed, Jorge and Tadeu acknowledged them the way folk acknowledged the inevitability of flies. They waved their arms in exasperation. The old men mistook the waving arms for a greeting and waved back.

o

Armando moved his brush with a languorous sweeping motion that carried the weight of age. Dust drifted above his head in a dark cloud. He yawned. His dentures slipped, revealing bare pink. He clacked his dentures back in place with the tip of his tongue.

"These kids today aren't of the same stripe as we were, Senhor Osório, are they?"

"Nope! Look at them." Senhor Osório motioned with his chisel-sharp chin, pointing to where the café patio opened in a garden of colourful parasols. The music blared from across the road.

"Strong bones and fresh legs idling away on those chairs. God gives nutshells to the weak of teeth." Armando slid a protecting cloth around the heel to save the pristine white socks from smudging. "In our time would anyone have caught us making shade long enough to kill a daisy, Senhor Osório?"

"Never!" Senhor Osório, in protest, lifted his cane, an ever-so-slight motion of intent to hammer the wood on the ground. The effort resulted in a barely audible squish.

"We would be running up and down the fields thinking up trouble for Senhor Esteves, poor devil, heaven keep him in the peace of the Lord."

Both men blessed themselves and kissed the tips of their fingers.

"That soul carried a heart tougher than a plum pit. Grew enough fruit to give the whole town the runs and yet he let it fall to a sea of mush. Never once did he sweeten a beggar's day with an apple." Senhor Osório lifted his eyes to the sky, striving to spot his memories floating among a vaporous cloud.

Armando stopped buffing Senhor Osório's shoes with his flannel rag. "Remember the year we stole his cherry crop to show him who carried more juice upstairs?" He pointed to his head with his thumb.

Senhor Osório's eyes sparked with memory. Ti Esteves' rage, a milestone in the lore of the town. As boys, they had planned the trouble months in advance while their parents turned a conspiring eye. Bands of youngsters had awaited the new moon before climbing the wall to Ti Esteves' orchard. First they distracted the two German shepherd dogs at the house gate with the pig Osório had stolen from his father's butcher shop. Their jaws occupied, tearing at the meat, the dogs never lifted their heads to bark. Ti Esteves was known to starve his dogs. "To build their ferocity," he claimed. "More likely to hunt for their food, less likely to be lenient with trespassers."

The sun drifted behind a building and cast a shadow half-way across the road. Old recollections crossed their eyes. Senhor Osório and Armando sat, looking up at the movie screen of the sky, inebriated by the images of the rusted reel.

"It took us less than an hour to undress the cherry trees."

The images, wrinkled and scarred, warped by time and much use; the blanks, begging to be adorned with fantastic embellishments.

The next day Osório's father had banged on Ti Esteves' gate demanding compensation for his murdered pig, victim of a savage and cowardly attack during its peaceful night stroll through the village. The pile of bones at Ti Esteves' gate proved the slaying instincts of his beastly dogs. "Should feed your dogs properly so their hunger doesn't snatch the innocent through the gate."

Reluctant, Ti Esteves had reached into his pocket, also promising thereafter a weekly order of bones from Osório's father. Ti Esteves, under his breath cursing his luck, chained the gate and walked into his shed, bringing out a ladder to harvest his fruit trees. The days to follow, he worked through the night, shooing the bats and picking the plums, pears and apples yet to ripen. The orchard stood naked and lonely for the remainder of the summer.

o

Jorge and Tadeu sank deeper into their seats. They had dragged their chairs behind the speakers, into the patio's back corner, where a sliver of sunshine still warmed the day. Rings of smoke circled their bodies. Empty peanut shells collected around their feet. Now and then, they rose from their chairs, visited the washroom and ordered another round of beers. The view offered nothing but their grandpas across the road.

"Man, can you imagine spending your life in this prison?"

"Once you're domesticated anything goes." Tadeu held his breath after a puff. His eyes widened.

"Give me a toke." Jorge stretched out his hand.

"Can't wait to escape this pit."

They threw their heads backwards and stared at a cloud drifting west, going places. They gazed at the green hills rising around them.

"Ever climb that peak?" Tadeu asked, lifting his eyebrows to point it out to Jorge.

"You crazy!" Jorge stared at Tadeu sideways, his face contorted in horror.

Tadeu nodded in agreement, stared at the incandescent tip of his toke.

"Yeah! This is high enough for me, that's for sure."

For the duration of a handful of peanuts they remained silent.

"Say, we pay a late night visit to the record store again?" Tadeu suggested, brushing broken peanut shells from his jeans.

"Yeah, it's been a while, I'm low on new tunes."

Jorge and Tadeu sat straight on their chairs and scrutinized their old grandpas with the curiosity of crowds at a zoo. In their eyes, the men resembled black flies drowsing on door steps where a beam of sunshine has landed. Jorge and Tadeu felt sorry for the creatures, resigned to their fate, living in a world that ceased to have a use for them, their footsteps moving slower with every passing year. The old men sat in their unvarying garments, the sad, depressing colours of dust. Their hair, a uniform sparse white against bare flesh, and short, unduly short.

"Wonder what they do all day?"

"Count flies for the government census!"

"Holy smokes, do those two ever live in the past."

"A few of their tales aren't that bad. Sort of cute."

"How would you know?"

"Caught a word here and there."

Tadeu flipped shelled peanuts with his thumb towards an abandoned neighbouring table. He attempted to score the peanuts into the half-full pint sitting on the table top.

"Poor old geezers can't even set up a stereo," Jorge said, shaking his head.

"That's true," agreed Tadeu. A dull plopping sound announced a successful peanut throw. A wry smile of accomplishment filled his face.

The boys looked at the old men with their stooped bodies unable to stand up to the riddles of modernity, day after day their shoulders weighed down with more questions, more doubts.

"We had to teach ourselves about the machine world, all right. We could even teach them a thing or two," Jorge continued. "Who cares about what seeds to bury on what shine of the moon anyway?"

o

Senhor Osório dropped a trickle of coins into Armando's hand. Armando accepted them with a respectful nod, wiped his hands on his smudged trousers. He tucked his brushes inside his shoeshine box.

"Come on, Armando, let's have a sip of wine. It's on me."

Senhor Osório stood and disappeared inside the dim tavern, returning soon with a bottle, two mugs and a bowl of salted lupini beans.

Red wine swirling inside the mugs, Armando and Senhor Osório watched the youths across the road, partly in awe, partly in fear.

"They all look alike under that woolly mane." The men nodded their heads in agreement. "Begging for a shearing, too," added Armando. They chuckled.

"A waste, sitting all day, a pity, numbing their lives on those drugs." Senhor Osório tilted his mouth backwards and emptied his mug in one gulp.

"Funny thing, but at home, my grandson doesn't stop long enough to warm up a seat. Can't pry a word out of him unless he is asking for coin."

Senhor Osório filled his palm with pickled lupini beans and proceeded to squeeze them, one by one, between his thumb and forefinger, out of their yellow skins and into his mouth.

"And of course you boot him onto the fields to hill potatoes and earn his thirst."

Armando shrugged and squeezed a few lupini beans in his mouth too.

"Well, silver will just weigh down my pallbearers," he confessed, avoiding the look in Senhor Osório's eyes.

Senhor Osório loosened the black tie on his neck and, now that they sat in the shade, at the end of the day, he rested his hat on his lap. Yellow lupini skins, blown from their mouths, piled around their feet.

"Too many choices today, Armando. Sheep can't make up their minds without a collie around. We knew our place, then." Senhor Osório whistled and, slightly lifting the empty bottle from the table, called inside the tavern for reinforcements.

A motorcycle swung across the road and slid to a stop a few paces from the two men.

"Hey, ready to go somewhere?" Without waiting for an answer, the boy accelerated to deafness and disappeared in a cloud of dust.

The men bit their lips. A sadness gathered around their rumpled eyelids. Their heads nodded gently, pondering.

"White hair doesn't command respect anymore," Senhor Osório mumbled, rubbing the dust from his eyes. "They think knowing how to fidget with trinkets means understanding something about life."

They were silent for a time before Senhor Osório continued.

"There was a time when they liked the view from our lap and sat listening to our stories. After they learned to run they never stepped nearby again." Senhor Osório frowned, scratching the ground with his cane. "Now we are no better than any old flea-infested dog."

"Once they begin walking it's mostly away . . ." confirmed Armando.

In the distance the church bells echoed through the evening air, announcing the end of another hour. An hour not unlike the one to come.

"Senhor Osório, ever thought about trying one of those motorized contraptions?"

"Nay, Armando. Those things move too fast for my old bones."

"Yep. Best to leave those modernities to the new roosters living without the curse of old bones."

"If only the winters weren't as cold!" said Senhor Osório.

"Or the fog didn't cut as deep!" Armando added with a nod of approval and a tap on his left knee. "Or the meat wasn't as tough!" he continued, clacking his dentures.

"And the distances weren't as long!" Senhor Osório sighed and rapped his cane on the dusty ground.

The old men, mugs in hand, minds heavy with wine, sat on the town square curbstone fermenting more batches of memories. They scratched their bulging bellies and shifted their cumbersome bodies with the awkwardness of expectant mothers. They watched the dust settle on their black trousers, watched it with longing. Each gulped another mouthful of wine.

"The times, yes, the times."

"That was the good life, Armando. Wasn't it?"

"Of course! A full life, even if those seedlings across the road don't think anything of it."

"Cheers!" The men clinked their mugs and gulped them in a quick throw.

Senhor Osório rubbed his chest, released a burp.

Armando's gaze followed the sun fading behind the green hills; it ended a day's journey, travelling from one end of the road to the other. The shadows filled his empty mug and, in time, crawled up his body, spread to the rest of the road.

THE TABLE

Smoke spirals from the mouth of the chimney, turns into a bruised cloud.

I approach the tumbledown house, stop at the stone washing tank by the entrance, stooping under its plastic pipe to quench my thirst. The cool spring water tastes of the earth, drips from my chin. I readjust the heavy package under my arm; the heel of my shoe pushes open the splintered door. The rusty hinges creak.

"Hello! It's your guardian angel."

I stand at the door adjusting my eyes to the dark.

"Also known as my son, the pest," she says, with a cheerful look from her low stool by the hearth.

I walk in with a smile and kiss her on each cheek. The skin, dry and weathered, the scraggly hairs, no longer shaved or thinned, graze my lips.

"No good wind can bring you this early on a Sunday!"

I force a polite laugh. I am yet to remove my jacket, and already she has me on the defensive.

"Look what I brought!" I lift the package under my arm — an easy-to-assemble pine veneer table from Ikea.

I open the door wider. The light flowing in joins forces with the glow from the fire and highlights the package. She squints.

"Another one of your modernities. Anything real under the cardboard wrapping?"

She huddles over the fire, fans more smoke than flames. In the woodbox, I notice the fresh pile of pine needles and twigs gathered for kindling.

"Up early, I see." I highlight my surprise by raising my eyebrows, then close the door.

Undeterred by a cast-confined foot, compliments of a rotten rung on her fig tree ladder, she has been up and about with her chores, convincing her body life must carry on. I admire her resilience. Any life blow only fires up her resolve to find her feet faster. I shake my head in worried exasperation.

On the iron trivet over the fire, a cauldron of boiling water gargles its hunger for the peeled potato, carrot, and turnip in the colander at her feet. The gas stove I bought her collects dust in the corner. "Nothing beats cornbread baked in a wood-burning oven," she would remind me every time I asked, until I quit asking. I sling my tie and jacket onto the back of her empty rocking chair. The chair sways.

"It's a brand new kitchen table, Mother. Your old one doesn't even sit right anymore. It's hard enough to eat your peas without having to chase the plate around the table."

"That's all right, Son. Better than chasing fancy ideas that we can never put our fork to."

I chuckle. My eyes adjust to the dimness. I step around the room with care, sniff the cornbread cooling on the table. This cornbread recipe will disappear with her. In this age, rare is the bread made by a bare hand passing on the human touch that nourishes another.

I tear a chunk of the loaf and bite into its crisp coat.

"Hmmm . . . Hmmm," I rumble, tilting my lips from side to side in accented pleasure.

That pleases her and she smiles.

"Nothing in the world beats the taste of your bread."

"Of course, it's the skin and sweat of my hands rising in that dough. That's what makes the soul of this loaf."

And she is right. Machine-made bread cannot pass itself to the next generation, cannot ensure the matrix of taste and nurture preserved. Today as she does every week, she offers to teach me how to make the cornbread.

"If I could find three idle hours in my week, I would go more often to the toilet. As it is, Mother, when I get home from the bank I want to put my feet up with a drink in hand. I'm not eager to take on another project. Sorry."

She harrumphs and turns her back, pretending to busy herself with shuffling and tidying up the embers at her feet.

I clear my throat, cough a little.

"That city is no good for your lungs, son."

I shrug, look around for a change of subject.

"We've got to do something about this floor. There are holes the size of fists. One day, you'll fall through and land in the wine cellar."

"Same mouse-sized holes you grew up with, lad. Should know them by heart now after years of spying on your cousin and his girlfriends, dropping beans on their heads."

I dislike being reminded of my less-than-proud moments from childhood.

"I know, I know. Let's assemble the table, then."

"Nothing wrong with the one I've got!"

"It's old, stained. It's had its time."

I kneel down, check the hinges under the table top. Underneath, I spot a carved heart. Inside, my own name and Ana's. My first love. I blush, remembering our first kiss under this table, shielded from the all-knowing eye of God. Or at least that was how I eased her fears and convinced her to kiss me.

"Who built your table anyway, and where does it come from?" she persists, quartering potatoes into the colander.

"How am I supposed to know who made it? Some assembly line somewhere, like everything these days. India. China. Who knows, who cares? Don't ask crazy questions, Mother."

"You dare bring a table inside my walls when you don't know in whose hands it's been? Today's furniture isn't worth fire smoke."

Outside, as if in agreement with her, the wind returns an unwanted grey cloud down the smoke hood. I cough, wave the smoke away from my eyes. My head brushes the blood sausages suspended from the rim of the hood. I stoop over the open hearth and look up to inspect a cracked roof tile revealing a sliver of blue sky.

I sigh, bite my lip.

"That table isn't welcome under my roof, son, not as long

as I'm around to say so." Irritated, she feigns anger and hurls a carrot. I catch it, bite into its firm flesh. She carries on. "I still remember trampling through the hills on my grandfather's back to harvest the oak." She points toward the cornbread on the table that sits under red painted shelves filled with jars of flour, black beans, pasta. "Even helped him sand the legs. A good kind man he was."

I tear off another chunk of cornbread. It tastes sweeter the second time. The deep wrinkles of hard crust crackle inside my mouth. Something real for the teeth to chew on.

My mother places her paring knife by her foot, adjusts the wooden pin holding the bun on her head.

"Trampling through the woods with my grandfather was as good a treat as a trip to the fair. In the woods, he taught me the call of the partridge, the cry of the fox." She stirs the broth — enough soup for the entire week. It will turn sour by then but she will not waste a drop. I hear the plock, plock of the carrot chunks leaping into the boiling water. Smells good with the garlic and olive oil. Slices of green beans will find their way last.

"And once," she resumes, "my grandfather offered my sister and me a choice of birthday presents. Any toy from the fair or a piece of his woods. My sister picked a guitar, I, the woods. Good old man he was!"

"Come on, Mother. Don't be stubborn. We aren't in the dark ages. There are plenty of modern and practical things around that could make your life easier."

"Probably why we don't hear much laughter in this world anymore. Not much practical use for it."

Maybe she is right. I can't remember the last time I was en-raptured by laughter. Maybe I have forgotten how or no longer have the leisure. With my pocket knife I cut the straps hold-ing the cardboard wrapping the table. I show her the glossy veneer and glide my hand over the smooth surface.

"Nice plastic top to clean. Always shiny. Not like these grooves on your tabletop, trapping old stuff, a haven for bac-teria and disease." I trace a groove with my fingernail. Crumbs emerge.

"That dent on the side," she says, not even needing to look, "belongs to you. Stubborn as a rock in your youth. But that day you sure crumbled."

I run the tips of my fingers over the dent, noticing the faint red stain.

"Running like a mad goose away from your father's belt after you stole the lark's eggs from their nest in the fig tree. Had to sew you up good myself. In those days no such thing as hospitals nearby."

Always a quick answer tucked deep in her red apron. I sigh and leave the bundle by the door so she has a few days to di-gest the idea. At least it will not rot. I sit beside her, pick up the hatchet at my feet, and split more kindling from the small logs, watching the flames bounce. The encrusted layers of soot have built a thick second skin, fossilized rivulets over the face of the iron trivet.

"Maybe I'll give the table to Ti Toneca," I say, looking from the corner of my eye at her.

She stares at the fire. Her hands slice each green bean to a half-length. They split open in her hand, becoming a two-petal flower before they disappear in the boiling cauldron.

"It'll be of no use where he's gone now. A whole week be-fore they found him."

I open my mouth and skip a few breaths. My father's only

surviving friend now also gone. An inevitable countdown. I thought I had grown immune to my mother's weekly necrology reports but I am shocked at his death and wonder what he died of.

I never liked him much after he lifted me by the ear at the country fair when I refused to hold my father's hand as other kids did with theirs, telling him he was deformed and that my friends called him a coward for not marching to the war and fighting for his country. Ti Toneca was pulling back his other hand to strike me with his knuckles when my father told him to let it run under the bridge. Placing a coin in my hand, he told me to go on my own and enjoy the rides.

"If Ti Toneca had not been as stubborn as a leaking tap and had moved in to the old folks' place like his children wanted him to —" I begin to say when she interrupts me.

"He sure couldn't look after himself very well, but he showed plenty of pride. They found him with a grin on his face, in the bed where he was born. Not many of us can say that much."

"Same grin he had when wobbling down the road kissing the bottle under his armpit?" I say and instantly regret it.

She pretends not to hear.

"A fine man he was who stood by your father against the venomous tongues. A day never passed without him saying, 'This is a village of morons. No braver man than yours graces this god-forsaken place.'"

I too remember this refrain when we crossed paths. And the vinho verde breath wrapping those words.

I rest the hatchet on the stone edge of the open hearth. The knell resonates over the crackling flames. I meander through the kitchen, hum a little, tighten the hinges on the cupboards with my pocket knife. I know she will not consent to nailing boards over those holes on the floor. At her age, any change in her daily territory is disconcerting. They are not mouse-sized holes. They are baby rabbit-sized. Every crack on the wall, warped utensil or stick of furniture in this house are old, faithful companions weathered by time, and she knows them intimately. Nothing will be discarded without heartache.

"I hear Ti Gustava decided to give the big city a try after all. Gusto says she's pretty happy in the old folks' place at the end of our street."

"That so! You and your cat-purring talk. The poor woman couldn't say a word with her left side frozen after the enstroke-ment. How could she say 'no'? Did Gusto forget to mention she kneed the ambulance attendant's dangling figs with her good leg?"

She slaps her thigh, laughs. My forced cough rings loud. I hope one day to find the words to tell her I appreciate her feistiness. It stirs my own divinely induced apathy and awakens me to everything I need not accept, including God's will.

"Mother, you complain the icy washing tank water burns your fingers, the foggy mornings rip your joints, and it's harder to get out of bed with each day. Well, that new place down the street does your washing for you. Dishes too. There will be other people your age to talk to about the good old times. And don't underestimate central heating at your age. Imagine, heaven year-round inside your room."

She pokes the coals and fans up the fire. A cloud of smoke surrounds her.

"What am I going to talk about to people I haven't known any younger in their lives? Leave me here to die among walls that know my secrets."

Is she attempting to distract me by tossing me fresh bait?

I want to ask about those secrets; however, that is not why I am here today.

"Come on Mother, I live an hour away. And since you're too stubborn to put in a phone, something could happen and we wouldn't know for days. Do you want to follow the fate of Ti Toneca, dead for a week before they found him?"

"Those places are good for people without family. I've got family."

"Places are smaller these days and people don't have the leisure to look after the old anymore," I say in the low tone of an apology.

The crackling of the flames echoes in the silence. I look around. It is not that modern dwellings are smaller now. They feel smaller. This house is a quarter of the size of my apartment and I do not remember it feeling tiny in my childhood. I am running out of arguments to convince her to move. I wish she behaved like most mothers, thankful for any crumb of attention, accepting the realities of this century. No time. No space. No money. A century of nothings. When I am around her, my guilt flourishes, fertilized by her resistance to my efforts to help, by her reminders that she does not look forward to the unavoidable compost heap of old age homes. I might sleep better if she went along with the script. At least, we could feign the civility of resignation and carry on with our respective silent discontent.

I tear off another chunk of cornbread and ask her if she set aside any loaves for the grandchildren. She nods.

"Yes, and where are the children anyway?"

"I left them in their pyjamas, watching morning cartoons. Hardly see them myself. Already in bed when I get home."

She shakes her head in blatant disapproval and tells me she worries about my children spending their days in front of TVs, growing paler by the day. "Bring them to the country to earn some colour in the sun."

I tell her life seems complicated nowadays. "Hard to pull the children away from TV without them hating me. I do worry about their health, though."

"An old crow like me isn't as colourful as those cartoons, and I sure don't move as fast."

"Or climb ladders or heal broken bones as fast either." I add a jab to my cause.

She continues without looking at me. "But I know a little magic that TV doesn't." She turns to me with a wide smile and winks.

I regret my jab. For a time we listen to the crackling of flames.

"I'm sorry," I say.

She reaches for the wicker basket tucked under the kitchen sink and picks up where she had left off the weaving of a garlic braid.

"Wanna give me a hand?"

She knows braiding garlic is my favourite farm relaxant. I bite one of the green tops, savour the sweet perfume, and let my hands tango with the reeds.

"Did those seeds I gave you come up?"

"Didn't have the time, Mother."

She looks at me sideways, evidence she does not believe me.

"A good wet year for the greens, wasn't it?"

I nod. She bites her lower lip.

"I remember you lifting your suitcase onto the bus, a clay pot under one arm, seeds tucked in your breast pocket, swearing you would rather die than go without your favourite fava beans."

"That was a long time ago," I protest.

"You couldn't wait to leave and make better money to retire sooner in life, retire to a patch of land and a dozen beehives humming on a south slope."

I resent being reminded of moribund dreams. My breath stops. My right shoulder clenches. Another trip to the physio-therapist tomorrow.

"Lives today are like leaves in autumn. They fly with the prevailing wind," I offer as an excuse.

After only ten minutes around my mother, I begin to sound like her, speaking in farming aphorisms. I can see it in her face, she is more comfortable with me when we share the language of the land.

"Autumn leaves are dead, son. That's why the wind can toss them around. We're birds, not leaves. Arms stretch like wings to steer our course in the sky." She flaps her arms to illustrate her point. "I could look after the children. You could renovate the house. The air is crisper here."

I sigh, thinking of my family of four, crowded in the upper floor of a condominium apartment. The conflict of wills. Two bathrooms under permanent occupation. And we enjoy more space than most in Porto.

"You and I don't know how to live with each other anymore, Mother."

"Never too old to remember. Wouldn't need to worry about each other. Everyone within sight, within earshot as your father used to say."

I take another small, digestible bite of a garlic green. After chewing it to a paste I let it linger in my mouth. The skin of my fingers glows red, highlights the friction of the weaving stalks.

"Eva and the children would die of boredom."

I sidestep the matter of her and Eva not seeing eye to eye. My mother still blames her for taking her only child away in her old age. Perhaps her point is valid and it's easier to bear life with more people around. I am surprised my fingers remember how to braid the garlic tops without looking at the pliable green stems. I am not far behind her pace. The garlic braids will hang in the drafty barn to complete their cure until they become papery and wrinkly.

"Do you remember dying of boredom growing up?"

I cannot say I did. Remembering the old days, of watching a spider weave its web or racing pine bark boats down the irrigation ditches, still brings a sweetness to my chest.

"People no longer spend enough time together to entwine their roots. At the slightest puff of frost they're blown away without a thought. Patience and tolerance were thrown away with the oxcart."

It is true. My children, trapped in the apartment, nowhere to run, not even in the neighbourhood park the size of a postage stamp. Everyone needs to run away a little, every day. Their friends live at the other end of town and I am too busy to chauffeur them. Eva complains she never finds time to watercolour after standing eight hours at the lab and herding two wound-up children around the home. Now and then the word *countryside* surfaces in our conversations and soon falls away, seeds scattered in a parking lot.

I imagine having weekends on the farm, resuscitating the vineyards to full bloom and giving the house a facelift, an opportunity for the family to adjust to the countryside and to each other. Feet slow and steady on the farm, finding the time to ask about the walls that cradle those secrets. Maybe then I would find the parts of myself I left hiding inside the walls, prompting my memory and releasing the stories before time will turn them to dust.

"Your father used to say happiness is not a place that one catches a bus to, happiness is the people you build your life with. He would rather have died than be taken away from his roots and his loved ones."

She picks up the hatchet and shaves paper-thin curls of wood from a split log. She tells a story:

"The day the conscription officials arrived at the door to take your father to the African war, he poured them two glasses of burgundy and sat them down at the oak table." Her tone is grave as she points her chin to the corner. "You were wrapped onto my back and sleeping through it all while I sat on this stool trembling and pretending to peel the same carrot over and over for the pot of soup on the fire. You had weak lungs. We were terrified you wouldn't see your first birthday. Your father asked them what good he would be away from his young wife and a sick newborn, both sure to starve without an extra pair of hands on the land. The officials smirked as if they had heard it all before and told him they did not make the laws. Did he want to go of his own free will or dragged in handcuffs? They tossed the handcuffs on the table, right where the cornbread sits now." She tilts her head toward the table. "Without a word your father picked up the hatchet from the woodbox and chopped off his index finger on the tabletop. He offered the finger to the officers, asking them if that 'qualified as sufficient proof he could not pull a trigger or did they require his whole arm?' He had the saw in his hand by then. The youngest official, poor fellow, passed out right there and then. The older one nodded in respect and, without another word, carried his mate down the hill on his shoulder. After that we worked this farm and never left you alone for a moment."

Ashamed that I had never noticed, I walk to the table and find the slash in the wood. It's there, subtle now, filled with crumbs, weathered by time. A dark, fading stain surrounds it. I look for my own stain next to the dent at the edge of the wood top. My fingertips trace old grooves in the table, deep, long, short, shallow.

I want to ask her the story behind each one.

THE RED SKIRT

The plate twirled in the air before shattering against the glazed tile floor. Maria, wet dishtowel in hand, bare feet dull from the cool tiles, feigned shock. Dona Branca, peeking through the venetian blinds at a crowded sky threatening thunder, stormed into a rage, her silence destroyed.

"Butter fingers! Clumsy creature. Ah . . . good for nothing!"

Maria dropped her gaze and waited for an end to the deluge of words, words as familiar as the smell of the thorny pineapple cache hanging just above her head. Nevertheless, she preferred Dona Branca's words to the unbearable wall of silence.

o

Iron pots to scrub, ebony chairs to dust, chandeliers to shine, zebra skins to beat, soups to simmer, and never able to satisfy Dona Branca's meticulous standards.

Maria's mother had reminded her with unrelenting frequency of how easy they had it: "Want to end up like cousin Fátima?! Ah ... if only you had tasted the hardship of blister-making work. Just watch poor Fátima labouring on Senhor Ernesto's plantation, earning rivers of sweat, mountains of worry, all for money that barely tricks her hunger. We're lucky Dona Branca takes such good care of us and asks for so little." Maria would roll her eyes and continue to iron the underwear or to polish a doorknob, humming against the insurmountable demands.

Remembering her mother's charcoal eyes, her raised finger stabbing the air, Maria trembled. The brief apparition, the company, comforted her in these moments when she clashed with Dona Branca. In the beginning, the apparition of her mother had often flashed her stern look; however, by now, she was losing voice and strength.

o

If it were not for Dona Branca what would become of her, a creature who couldn't do anything right? When would she ever learn? Eyes shut, she dammed the steady current of rumbling words that assailed her.

"Only my good Christian heart stops me from sending you to the streets. What would you do? Monkey tricks for bananas? Useless creature!" Dona Branca cast a last glance at the storm. With fastidious fingers, she tightened the rod on the blinds to shield the sombre house from light. Then, aided by her cane, Dona Branca shuffled her way back to the rocking chair.

"Better off doing the chores myself!" She sat, straightened her narrow shoulders and lifted her chiselled chin. Her hands rested on her immaculate linen dress, hands and dress competing for paleness. Never once had she allowed the fiery passion of the sun to taint her skin. "This is a damned country," she often said. "The very home of the devil. A curse is what this infernal heat is. Yes, a curse that unveils the flesh and stirs a body's sins to the surface." Dona Branca ensured thick concrete walls stood between her and the devil, yet not even concrete succeeded in repelling the stray and devilish whispers of muggy breath that infiltrated her home.

The relentless fans became her only allies.

o

"I'm sorry, terribly sorry. It won't happen again," mumbled Maria, her unsteady hand rattling the porcelain shards in the dustpan.

"It won't happen again! It won't happen again! Sometimes I wonder why the Lord placed your kind on earth! Hurry. Order the gardener to cover the birds of paradise before the rain tears them to pieces," Dona Branca said, retrieving the .22 slung over the back of her rocking chair. "And be sure to return in a breath," she added. Maria had already disappeared.

o

After the wings of malaria had carried her husband away, Dona Branca, consumed by nightmares of home invasions, bought the .22 to protect her from wild beasts, bandits, pests, cannibals, cataclysms — an endless list of dangers known to roam the continent, a list recited every day to Maria after Dona Branca glued another newspaper clipping to the album of disaster stories stored under her rocking chair. This morning, the breakaway story of a zoo elephant stomping through a village and destroying a farmer's corn crop occupied her clipping scissors.

The week after becoming widowed, Dona Branca had every entrance door steel-reinforced and deadbolted, her nightmares of the outside menaces reaching such magnitude that she had also arranged the delivery of daily staples to their front steps. After that resolution, it was rare the day Maria glimpsed daylight. Pulled by invisible strings, she went about her daily chores, a silent Dona Branca periodically gravitating into her sphere. Two astral bodies locked within each other's magnetic orbit, the silence interrupted only when Maria, tired of the quiet, dropped a plate or porcelain doll to trigger Dona Branca's rage.

○

"God is witness to the countless hours I've wasted, toiling to educate you. In return, I receive this miserable behaviour." When Maria returned from the garden she heard Dona Branca's continuous lamenting.

In the early days, Dona Branca had sat Maria in the kitchen, legs dangling far from the floor, teaching her needlepoint. "A very beautiful virtue for any proper girl to cultivate." Dona Branca taught Maria to sew a complete playhouse, a red chimney, a window that swung open to a view of pink carnations as Maria bent in concentration over the needle, with strained eyes and prickled fingers.

"I have pulled my hair out attempting to give you an appreciation for life's finer things, but you are such an ingrate, your mind always elsewhere."

Maria pressed more firmly on the soft cloth buffing the cupboard door that already reflected her gritted teeth.

"Look at the hour, girl. We don't have all day to spend on a door. It's time for your piano lesson. Hurry to the living room before the day runs away on us."

There had been piano lessons all along, her mother ecstatic over Dona Branca's interest in educating Maria, and daydreaming of her child one day fluent in the ways of the people who owned crystal chandeliers and the adorable ebony boxes that spilled music while perfect porcelain dolls in white lace dresses swirled on their toes.

Maria, now facing the grand piano, entangled by the complexities in the Vienna Waltz, exasperated the sensitive ears of Dona Branca, who stood behind her marking tempo with a finger on her shoulder. While she bent over the white and black of the piano keys, surrounded by the permanent dimness of the living room, Maria's mind fled to past mornings when a barely awakened sun had hurried both her and her mother to the market.

o

Maria and her mother, baskets hungry for bananas, passion fruit and pineapples, sang while scurrying along the seawall that barred the blowing sand from conquering the streets.

"The early salty mist is good for the lungs": her mother's words followed by a series of cavernous coughs and a fleeting rest. Although Maria was forced to wear an ankle-length white linen dress, her waist strangled by a pink bow and her toes constricted by matching vinyl shoes, the singing and the walking remained the radiant part of Maria's day.

"Maria, in this life we must do as we are told. There are people who know better and are here to teach us a better life. See . . . all servant eyes are on you. They envy your white clothes and your luck. Don't let them down!" Maria was not oblivious to the stares following her down the boulevard and wanting to walk in her shoes. Despite her enjoyment of being centre stage, as soon as she caught sight of the cheerful wooden shack halfway to the shoreline, she pretended to have her shoes untied. "Hurry Maria, we must return before Dona Branca wakes up," her mother would say even as she rested on one of the red iron benches scattered along the boulevard, grateful for the opportunity.

Maria, not listening, savoured the festival of orange, yellow, and green that decorated the fishermen's shack. Around the house, Dona Branca took pride in her choice of serious colours, beige as festive a tinge as she would allow herself to display. On the beach, children clothed in damp patches of sand climbed up the shack's roof, jumped, sprinted across the tide line and dove into the ocean where the crashing surf, without ceremony, repatriated them to the shore. She dared to imagine herself with them on the roof, the coarse air tasting of seaweed scraping her throat, the wind stirring clouds of grit that collected in the folds of her ears, the corners of her lips. Maria, already in trouble for sitting on the iron benches and wrinkling her precious garment, afraid of triggering further distress in her mother, never dared to embark on such an adventure. At other times, hurried along the boulevard, and out of the corner of her eye, Maria spied the children gathered around drums, singing and dancing, their laughter rolling on the sand. Their agile bodies swayed, music dripped from skin, glazed bodies sparkled in the sun.

That is where Maria travelled when Dona Branca demanded that she put her heart into the Vienna Waltz: the pounding of the surf drumming in her head drowned the cadence of Strauss.

o

Today, more than ever, Dona Branca resented Maria for not embracing the piano.

"No, no, like this. Are you listening to me, Maria?" Dona Branca sighed as her arthritic fingers stumbled across the black-and-white keys in an attempt to demonstrate the proper tempo of a chord.

Maria, eyes shut, hummed. Her arms hung by her side, her hands, not knowing what to say, fidgeted against her red woollen skirt, once her mother's and the only possession Maria had cared to hold on to. Her fingers picked at the yellow stains of past Sundays' rice curries, her mother's favourite; at the orange-browns of bleeding passion fruit, her own childhood breakfast favourite. Maria sucked on a finger. The sight of this old rainbow of stains quivered Dona Branca's lips first thing in the morning and set her irritable tone for the day.

"Are you listening to the proper tempo, Maria?"

In the whisper of Dona Branca's failing breath, the sign of Maria's relief appeared on the horizon. "Maria, you are a test to the Lord's patience."

Even the Mukarela Falls turned to a trickle in the dry season, Maria thought.

"Bless your heart, poor creature, appease the Lord, show

Him your repentance for your lack of gratitude. Do not sit there, go fetch the rosary."

As though fearing Dona Branca's words might blow forever away into the sombre vastness of the house, Maria sprang to obey them. She devoured the steps between her and the rosary with the appetite of youth, only halting at the imposing door that sealed Dona Branca's room from the rest of the world.

Maria studied the door. The upper panel depicted Saint Peter holding an oversized key at heaven's gate. The lower depicted flocks of angels blowing trumpets and staring in awe at Saint Peter. She did not understand the wonder that drew such attention to what was after all a plain key. "Useless burden to carry," she whispered and shook her head.

Maria stepped inside. Blinded by even deeper darkness, waiting for her eyes to adjust, she picked at her nose and, with impatience, rolled the snot between her fingertips. The dimness dissipated. She moved in tentative steps now, and as her hip brushed the dresser at the far end of the bed she pressed the smooth and round snot under the dresser's edge. The edge of the bed guided her body to the night table where the rosary dangled from a lamp. Maria wondered if Dona Branca would ever forgive her the day her mother had fallen sick. Unannounced, Dona Branca had arrived to inspect their room. "A clean place starves disease," she said in a tone suggesting her mother's illness might be attributed to lack of hygiene. As she ran her finger through the dust on Maria's cheap metal headboard, her gaze squeezed between Maria's bed and the wall, eyes bulging at the sight of years of pasted snot. Dona Branca shrieked and fled the room gagging, which translated for Maria into a full week of brushing walls, the magnitude of the work suggesting the whole house had been infected.

In haste, Dona Branca supplied her with additional hand-kerchiefs, which joined a rising pile under her pillow. Maria, enraptured by the embroidered colours, did not have the heart to soil a single one. "Mamma would have been upset had she known I saved that snot in a matchbox," she murmured, reaching for the rosary. That first evening of the brushing, while mixing Dona Branca's nightly milkshake, Maria had taken her time. Extra smooth. The following morning a good-spirited Dona Branca praised her for the first time in front of her mother. "A delicious milkshake, Maria. At last learning the secrets of the civilized. One day we will be proud of you."

On that last day, her mother smiled all day long.

o

"Maaaria!"

Dona Branca's scream, followed by the blast of her gun, pierced Maria's hovering thoughts. Rosary in hand, she raced to the kitchen where Dona Branca had returned to rest in her rocking chair. Livid, Dona Branca was aiming the .22 at the space between the stove and cupboard. Not again, thought Maria. Double doors. Double screens. Damn creatures still found a way in to torment Dona Branca. Maria stared at the bullet hole in the cupboard door, smelled the acrid gunpowder spreading through the kitchen. She sighed, annoyed by the prospect of repairing one more hole in that cupboard.

"Be-sure-it-is-dead!"

Maria walked to the sink. Underneath, a chemical arsenal stood in alphabetical parade. She selected the tallest, an orange canister labelled H-Bomb, and, aiming at the nothingness before her eyes, sprayed.

"Is it still moving?" whispered Dona Branca, lowering the .22 to her lap.

Maria, rosary wrapped on her wrist, reached for the broom, clumsily sliding it in and out between the stove and the cupboard before inadvertently catching and ripping the skirt's pocket with the end of the broomstick. Maria froze, wide-mouthed at the cloth now hanging from her hip.

"Come, come . . . on with your job," Dona Branca pressed.

Beads of sweat accumulated on Maria's brow with each frenzied and unsuccessful prod of the broom into the narrow space until the dazed black cockroach finally staggered out on his own.

"Kill it!" Dona Branca yelled.

Maria whacked the cockroach with the bushy broom. The cockroach stopped moving.

"This land grows armies of cockroaches. I cannot have a moment of peace. I am fortunate my husband left me the .22. If those miserable creatures can infiltrate this place, imagine being at the mercy of a stomping mad elephant." Dona Branca lifted her gaze from the wedding band she had been twirling in the palm of her hand. "Do not stand there staring at your dreadful skirt, girl. Go flush the filthy cockroach out of sight."

Maria kicked the cockroach into the dustpan and, imagining she carried a coffin, dispatched the invader to the bathroom, prepared to execute the sentence. Lifting the lid on the toilet, Maria noticed the cockroach's legs still moving, unwilling to quit, grasping for life. Overcome by an ache in her chest, Maria opened the window and released the cockroach. She pleaded to the fresh air to awaken the creature from its deathbed. "Even if you are not meant to survive, you should die among green grass and open sky where you belong."

Maria flushed the toilet and stared with a wry smile into the empty swirl.

o

Maria, rosary dangling from her hand, circled the mahogany table on her knees as instructed by Dona Branca, to build endurance for a future pilgrimage to Fátima. Maria's words leaped from Hail Marys to Our Fathers as effortlessly as a bee slips from flower to flower, hungry and searching. Rocking in her chair, Dona Branca, chin high and shoulders rigid, joined Maria in the singing pilgrimage along the rosary, her words solemn and grave. Maria's lips danced in devotion. In prayer, Maria stretched her sweet voice out of Dona Branca's reach. The sound filled the room to the rim.

"Hail Mary full of grace . . ."

Outside, the sky, stirred by the rising voice, spilled rain over the land. Drops pounded against the slanted roof and in the sacred refuge of her prayer Maria gazed upward and smiled at the music from the heavens, at the expressionless face of her mother who had nothing more to say. Dona Branca chased Maria's gaze. "At last heaven's waters shall drown this infernal heat." Dona Branca, elated in the moment of victory, prayed with additional fervour.

". . . and lead us not into temptation but deliver us from evil, cockroaches and cannibals."

Maria's mind, prompted by the rain falling, remembered the drum beats that sneaked into her room under the cover of night. She grinned and prayed on.

". . . as we forgive those who trespass against us."

o

Retreating to the haven of her room, away from Dona Branca's prying eyes and abrasive voice, Maria lay in bed, window open wide, her gaze nailed to the southern cross. The distinct aroma of fried snapper, seasoned in ocean mist and lifted by the evening breeze, trespassed the garden's whitewashed wall. As usual, the evening began tame. Murmured voices on the beach. Gentle tapping of drums one could mistake for one's heartbeat. Later, the contagious laughter and the glare of flames reaching for the moon. The scorched land releasing stored heat with passion. Charged bodies sang to clapping ocean waves while the drums enticed shadows to dance. The night erupted as songs soared and dwarfed the palm trees.

Maria rose from her bed and joined the invisible chorus. Her body a kite, the music, a gust of wind.

The summoning moon, starting its journey across the open night, peeked into Maria's room, full eye cast upon the far corner. Her mother's bed plain and bare, a tossed red woollen skirt abandoned in its lap.

THE GREEN AND PURPLE SKIN OF THE WORLD

Dear B,   Quinta da Garrida, courtyard
                                                           three weeks

The morning yawns and sighs in the lungs of the birds. I begin
the day on the front steps, in my bathrobe, blowing soap bubbles. The birds' harmonies melt the thin veil of frost covering
the ground to reveal the green.

  You phoned last night to say you won't be at Pearson airport
to meet me. You'll be in Victoria visiting your aunt.

In this corner of Europe the sun shines through a winter blue.
Oranges on the trees glow and kiwis shrivel on vines. All this
fruit doesn't tempt me to stay.

Since my last visit my father has relocated the blackbird cage to a more secluded corner near the garden wall. Perch to perch, the bird hops in a frenetic pattern when I approach the cage in my lilac pyjamas.

Have you noticed how the eyes follow the largest, the most colourful upward-floating bubble, and ignore the bubbles that drift downward? Sometimes a bubble floats near the ground, long after the others have burst. Bubble and ground meeting eye to eye.

As I pull the purple wand from the plastic bottle, a mere whisper creates exquisite round worlds. Is this what they mean by the Creator expanding the universe?

Beijos,
Shana

o

Dear Beloved,   Quinta da Garrida, graveyard
                                 one and a half weeks

I'm not needed today. A fierce wind blows streams of bubbles any time I lift the wand. They fly away in haste. I sit at the edge of my grandparents' grave. A hole sealed by smooth and heavy marble. Memories, three generations deep. The bubbles collide with marble crosses, attracted to the reflections in the smooth stone. In Canada, I've no graves to sit beside.

You phoned again. You'll be in Victoria because you've fallen in love. You plan to marry next month. He's moving in. You don't wish to discuss the matter.

Strange to see myself reflected in a bubble, travelling on the wind. A shock to find myself disappearing in mid-air with a pop. Have you ever stared at a bubble for an eternity only to realize it has already burst? Alive only in memory.

I shake the soap bottle. Blowing, blowing, I want to crowd the graveyard with bubbles. I want to see bubbles grow out of the wand, fill the air. Fill the air like a stream of tears.

On occasion bubbles float, attached. One smaller than the other. Together they encounter the blades of green on the ground. A comforting image.

I understand the urgency. You've passed forty. A bubble floats close to the barbed wire fence.

Beijos,
Shana

o

Dear Be loved,   Quinta da Garrida, motherland
                                   a week and two days

I think of my mother as I watch the wind lift a bubble over the roof. It flies away and out of sight. I hope it will be happy. I'd like to know its destination. There's a tall spruce behind the house. A spruce with fifty thousand needles. I imagine the bubble bringing a smile of surprise to a neighbour sitting in clouds of worry by a window.

My mother tongue is blunt now, a rusted tool unable to dig into the depths of the ground on which I walk. My old tongue has lost its magic. It no longer churns my thoughts into the words I once knew, thoughts that will bloom and bear the fruit planted in a distant childhood.

Home is any language I speak. Words of the heart unlock the doors and invite people in to touch the tender, most bloodied parts of my concealed self. Words carry me through the shadows, the gritty corners where I meet the unforeseen, and decipher the shadows' undefined contours.

I speak in the past and imagine the future. I'm not here.

Beijos,
Shana

o

Dear Be,   Quinta da Garrida, solstice
                                                      seven days

The cat lounges on the tile stairs, presses his black body against the terracotta vases, twice squeezing the warmth out of this day. He will count the rotations of the earth until the shadows arrive and announce it's time to beg for warm milk at the back door.

I've heard there are wands in the shape of hearts. I don't have the courage to inflate a heart that will encounter sharp edges.

Sometimes I save a bubble from crashing on the ground, catch it with my wand. The bubble clings, happy, holding on to the stillness. I blow it back up. It twirls and glistens. I catch it again before it falls. We are prisoners of one another. I can't leave without it dying. I blow it up. I catch it again. Each time the bubble becomes thinner and weaker.

Beijos,
Shana

o

Dear love, Quinta da Garrida, river
six days

Strolling by the river in late afternoon, I'm walking the winding road to the house of my childhood, the house of today. Rose vines spread along the whitewashed wall encircling the house. In summer, a plum tree leans over the wall and offers fruit to passersby. Now, the branches stand empty, nothing to give. My grandfather hoed the ground, planted the seed, watered the sapling, knowing he wouldn't live to taste its golden juices trickling down the corner of his mouth.

Someday I will walk up this road and there will be no one waiting with fresh flowers on the table. My words will stay in my stomach like a swallowed fishbone from childhood still stabbing me.

Two bubbles clash. Do they turn into one, larger and brighter? Do they float into each other's lives, smooth and beautiful? One bursts. A tender bleeding of purple in my retina only.

We no longer carry the words in our bodies until they ripen. Letter writing is nearly extinct. We respond with the deathly speed of a duel. The fruit is picked green. We are late for our next experience and swallow the fruit without tasting.

Beijos,
Shana

o

Dear Bee,   Quinta da Garrida, grandparents' farm
                                                a handful of days

There are blues, greens, and purples in a bubble. In any skin purple is a heavy tone that penetrates to the core.

A gentle breath shapes the bubble's skin. Light tickles its surface. Faith lifts the thinnest dream above ground. Happiness rises in the colour of a floating bubble. There will be an ending. Fear weighs, sinks a bubble to the ground. Is that why our baby didn't arrive?

My chest aches. Blow one, three, five times, blow in desperation, but no bubbles are born. My lips fail to find its perfect mould. My breath doesn't inflate another body with life. My hand trembles. My mouth opens. The silenced words escape.

A bubble's beauty exists in its groundlessness, in that vulnerable, tender place where light envelops the bubble. To touch ground is conclusion.

Every day I stumble in my mother tongue. The words aren't there. I remember the cork beehives nestled against the stone wall of the green, the terraced fields, where now there is only a highway. Standing by my side, alive, staring at the cars passing, my father says he's glad his parents didn't live to see the highway run over the farm.

Are my words buried under a new language or were they never there? I open my old heart with the key of a new alphabet, new sounds.

Language wraps the world in a thin, temporary veil.

Beijos,
Shana

o

Dear B-love,   Quinta da Garrida, garden
                                                          three days

Peaceful, I blow bubbles, relish the breeze that holds the bubbles forever in the air that determines their trajectory and pushes them toward nothingness. Astrologers say the day you're born shapes you, your life.

The cat has joined me. Feline joy jumps around the yard, claws the bubbles out of existence. Cats do what they do best. It's not pleasant to watch.

A bubble lands on a puddle, slides on its surface. Stops as if to stay, as if real. I wait for passengers to exit from the sides. Nothing happens.

The next bubble swells in the wand and bursts in my face. Wet spit cools my skin. Doubts of existence dissipate.

Beijos,
Shana

o

Dear belo, Quinta da Garrida, dark
two nights

Full moon. Cradled inside a bubble, in its belly, it rises and rises until there is no bubble, just a moon among the stars. A tinge of blue around the edges.

A blue moon is rare. I wish for a new century. I wish for gentleness, and to learn through laughter. The moon listens.

Last time we loved, you pressed me against your chest and held me in your gaze. For the sixth time in as many years you told me, nothing will ever happen that we don't decide together. Dropping me off at the airport you whispered, "Come back to me."

The subtle manner in which a bubble pops. A puff. Tear-shaped drops plunge downward. Early this morning I walked along the Rio Caima to the weir where I swam as a child. I gazed at an upstream rock, a place the brave swam to then lay basking in the sun. In those days, I believed the rock rose from the bottom of the world. Not today. Further up, around the curve, appeared the bridge from which my grandfather threw his children into the river so they would learn to swim.

You've never smelled the permeating shower of sweetness dripping from purple-skinned *uvas americanas*, dangling from the grapevines, a scent that sinks into the pores. Not even water will dilute it. You've never stood at the edge of my past, hand in hand, imagining me running through the grass to my lunch bag and hearing the crunch of my teeth sink into the hard crust of a corn loaf. My tongue whisks the air inside my mouth and shapes the thoughts.

There are sounds in my mother tongue your throat will never set free.

Beijos,
Shana

o

Dear Be,   Quinta da Garrida, the wall
                                                                one day

Soft lemon light rests on a bubble. A caress that polishes the colours. What courage to travel through the world so thin-skinned. A ray of light punctures the bubble. What willingness to be hurt. Does a bubble burst or does it open to the world? One moment there, the next imperceptible. Is this what monks mean by becoming one with the world?

Last week a neighbour invited his grandson to play with him. He stood the boy on the wall surrounding the house and he opened his arms. He smiled. The child jumped. The man stepped aside. Never trust anyone, he told him, wiping blood from the child's face. Again and again I see that boy climbing the wall and jumping toward those promised arms.

Beijos,
Shana

o.

Dear B, Quinta da Garrida, orchard
today

The bubbles flying high among the crows. The crows swoop and dive, approach the bubbles and cry. Their wings gather wind, swirl the bubbles. Birds and bubbles. A tango. I return today and the last six years won't be at the airport to catch me.

It's only January and the blackbird tosses its first crystalline notes into the air. Next to the well a flower waits for no one and bursts from the lips of the plum tree. Spring is early. Even here.
  Cherry and plum trees, fooled by the signs of warmth, show the world their tender petals. This is a predictable language. It's in the roots. They haven't been warned that times have changed. They slept through the winter. Some trees never shed their green leaves. Father fears another terrible year. Sudden frosts will sneak in through March and burn the skin of the world.

Beijos,
Shana

MY REAL MOTHER WOULD NEVER

I didn't plan on running away. It happened.

You stare at me from down the street, and when we cross paths, you turn and shake your head as I walk along, stuffed rabbit under my arm, rainbow-coloured sling bag bulging with my comfort blanket and my *Anne of Green Gables* book collection biting my shoulder. If you stop and talk to me I'll tell you, "My real mother would never do such a thing."

I'm dead sure my mother isn't my real mother. I've got eyes. I mean, look at us. I have dusty blond hair. Hers: black. At the wave pool I'm skinny and sink like a nail. She floats without trying. I have freckles. She doesn't. I hate smashed squash, she loves it.

And I'd rather know the truth now, thank you very much. Not like my best friend, Tilda, who only found out last week that she was adopted. She wanted to die. And why the wait 'til she is nine? How will she ever believe anything her parents-not-parents tell her again? I'm sorry for Tilda. I've also been trying to pull the truth out of my mother for weeks now.

o

Kurt swears he dropped her off from the car pool at 3:30. She's not in the playground. I phone Tilda's mother, surprising myself with the calmness of my voice, the steadiness of my breathing. "Hi. Mara's mom here. Have you seen my daughter?"

Twenty mothers later, I put the phone down and stare out the window. I thrust my finger into the soil of a potted plant and break a nail. The cemented soil would choke any root. The yellow leaves droop. It will cope. "Fig trees are resilient plants. Impossible to kill, even if you wanted to," the salesperson guaranteed. The poor thing hasn't seen a drop of moisture since finals started three weeks ago. Poor violets, too. With a pop I pull the cracked, dried soil from the pot. Skeletal stems poke out. It's my third try at growing violets. Why do beautiful flowers need so much extra care?

Can't call the police. It would be as good as saying goodbye to my daughter in the middle of her father's rehashed custody battle after I filed for enforcement of his delinquent payments. I imagine the lawyer pacing, gesticulating from one end of the courtroom to the other, firing words at my chest — bad mother, irresponsible, incapable, unloving, uncaring — bleeding me to tears.

I've told Mara not to answer the doorbell or the phone when

she's home alone. She knows she isn't supposed to leave for any reason whatsoever. There are so many weirdos out there.

o

I want my mother to worry. I hope she cries. Then again she may not notice or even care. She tells me all the time to get lost because I'm driving her crazy and she needs space. Well, I'm getting lost, all right. She's had plenty of warning. We fight every day. And every day I run and hide underneath the couch where it's dark. After a while she calls out to patch things up. "It's too quiet," she says. She's worried. I pretend I don't hear a thing. Serves her right, she can find me if it's that important. "Where are you? Are you hiding?" Her voice is out of breath. "Are you all right, sweets?" I don't budge. And then she gets angry, twice as mad. "Why didn't you answer me? Don't ever try that again. It scares the hell out of me." I think it would be a good thing to scare the hell out of her.

o

It's chaos in Mara's room. I know this isn't the time to be upset, but her messy habits still bug me. A maimed doll sprawled in the middle of the floor, a red-stained play bandage twisted in a knot around the head, a play cast on its hand. Her latest obsession, playing injured, drives me crazy. For an entire week she can carry her bandaged arm in a sling, acting as helpless as a two-year-old. Next week it's her hand, then her knee. She insists on wearing her bandage du jour to Safeway. Of course some old lady doesn't take long to ask what happened to the poor child's arm. And that's all she needs to fabricate a convoluted story about an accident. If I'm lucky, the story doesn't outlast my whole shopping circuit, otherwise I have to wait for her in the parking lot while she finishes her tale. It drives me wild. The old ladies offer her lots of sympathy and time to listen. There's no point in saying she can't play injured anymore because then she arrives from school with real injuries.

Mr. Carrot, her stuffed rabbit, isn't on his usual pillow hangout. And Speedy, her hamster, must know something I don't since he hasn't stopped racing his frantic wheel. The same irritating squeak that keeps me awake at night. There's an envelope on top of the cage. It's addressed to Tilda.

Dearest and goodest friend Tilda,

I'm leaving Speedy behind. Will you please take good care of him? I'll pay you once I get a job because I won't be getting my allowance now that I stopped helping with the chores at home.

Love
Mara

o

Here comes Freckle, Mrs. Tate's terrier, carrying a white envelope in his mouth, trotting past me without a blink of remembering. And there's his waggling tail at the end of the street disappearing into the corner store. I wait until Freckle comes out, folded newspaper in his teeth, trotting back, no time to waste on me, focused on the task, ears pointing home, eyes flashing: reward, reward, biscuit, biscuit. Often Freckle stops and lets me rub his ears and tummy. I love dogs. On my birthday I begged for one, but no luck. My mother suffers from allergies and her new boyfriend, Kurt, dislikes animals on leashes or in cages. Everyone owns a pet. He's weird.

He told me with super slow and careful words like he was teaching me a higher level of religion, "It's cruel to confine animals and make them food-beggars for the rest of their lives."

I put my hands on my hips and told him, "Same cruel as when my mother sends me to my room, no?"

"Never thought of it that way before," he laughed, ruffling my hair and messing it up again.

o

The year we got pregnant, Mara's father announced he liked dabbling in nature and we planted our first garden. He made a point of planting the beds himself, poking the seeds into the moist ground with his index finger. His horticultural interest peaked about the time the first sprouting heads reached for sunlight, bursting through the small cracks of fertile soil. Proud of his garden, he insisted on showing it off to visitors, tossing newborn Mara in the air among the tall potted sunflowers I had bought from the nursery. Such a delighted father.

The first blooming season passed and his interest in the garden waned. "Weak back, rusty knees." Complain. Complain. Fighting with the crabgrass wasn't for him. In fact anything to do with bending his knees seemed to take a toll on his health. First in the garden, then any sort of maintenance work: bathing the baby, changing diapers, or wiping vomit off the kitchen floor. Come summer, weeds choked the seedlings. He wasn't showing the garden off anymore.

o

I think I'll go into Sammy's to buy an ice cream sandwich. My favourite treat. It'll help my spirits. Why are you still following me? You think I don't know you are only pretending to buy a newspaper? You think I haven't noticed you hiding under those black sunglasses and toque? Sammy asks me where I'm going all by myself and I don't lie when I tell him I'm going for a sleepover. Which I am, I just don't know the exact over.

Grownups forget what it's like to be a kid. If you ask me, there's nothing worse. Well, unless you're a pet, like Speedy. I tell him to sit, I tell him to play dead. And he does even though no one believes me and Kurt shakes his head. I left Speedy behind because I'm afraid he might catch a cold and die. The pet store told me to make sure I took very good care of Speedy and to never leave him in the cold because a little cute thing like a hamster needs love and warmth.

One thing that's bad about being a kid is that no one asks what you think. "No one asked you for an opinion," that's what I'm told when I speak up and tell my mom what I think of her boyfriends. A real mother would want to know what her kid thinks of her boyfriends. But she doesn't even listen when we're supposed to be having a conversation about my day at school and how I hate Mrs. Peterson's squeaky voice. I talk, she nods her head a lot, says "right" and "of course, sweetheart." But when she says, "I see" and "yep" while reading a recipe book, I can tell she's somewhere else. People who listen, like her friend Carol, look me in the eye when I'm talking and they don't cook dinner and wash the dishes at the same time. Mom's mind hovers somewhere else, probably school, thinking about the next exam or the trouble at the peace meetings that Kurt started her in. When *she* stops to look me in the eye after I mouth off, I'm careful about what I say next.

At school they tell me I'm a chatterbox. Maybe because I can't stop telling everyone about Speedy running in the bathtub and sliding down the sides or hiding in the vacuum cleaner hose; telling about my parents sitting at opposite ends of the gym for my Christmas concert pretending they'd never met; or telling that I don't like Mom's new boyfriend pulling at his nose hairs at the kitchen table. When I get home I'm still a chatterbox. The day before yesterday I started in the hallway telling her about Tilda finding out she was adopted and how upset she was. She told me to be quiet 'cause she was studying for an exam. I had to, but I felt like singing at the top of my lungs just to bug her. I would, if I could. It's so dead when she is studying. She needs to concentrate so I can't hum, let alone sing. I have to tiptoe. When she was finished studying and cooking dinner I talked through the radio news, making sure I was louder, and she was all *yep* and *sures*, busy at the stove until she cranked the stereo and started dancing with a glass of wine in her hand. Maybe if my mom had listened I wouldn't have gone on and on. I yakked and sang too and accidentally broke a flower vase. She sent me to my room.

I talk a lot when it's dark, too. Since Mom got headphones for Christmas I just talk myself and Speedy to sleep and tell him a made-up story about a space travel hamster with a rocket that goes to explore a planet made of Swiss cheese.

o

I call British Columbia.

"Mom, I need your help." It's the first important thing I say after we go through the inanities of weather. "Mara ran away from home."

"But she's only nine."

"I'm not sure what to do here."

"When you ran away at thirteen I thought you were awfully young."

"I don't remember that, Mom."

"It still haunts me."

"What happened?"

"Only God knows what idea got wedged in your head. One day you were up and gone. No warning. You were always pulling some stunt to get attention so I knew you'd turn up. That evening Mrs. Polanski, five houses down the street, phoned me to say you were fine and that you could stay with her for the next little while. Six months later you were back. Do you remember Mrs. Polanski, dear?"

"Vaguely, that's all."

"Maybe for the better."

I can never remember much of my past. I envy the vivid stories people tell at parties about childhood summer vacations on lake cottages filled with laugher, ice cream, and family tickling. My life was in a dive then, that I know. And me, I was a snorkeller drifting underwater at the mercy of the currents, groping for direction, a slow lazy motion in the murky waters. I've collided with a fair number of shipwrecks, salt corroding their steel bones, their ghostly shapes. Terrifying shadows, a permanent out-of-focus picture of my past.

"Go pour yourself a nice G'n'T and relax, hon." The smooth clinking of ice precedes a quick gulp before she continues.

"Mara probably just went out to fetch ice cream since you don't let her have it at home."

I look sideways to the open closet mirror and shudder. I'm already holding a G'n'T in my hand.

o

My mother doesn't know what it feels like having no choice in what happens to me. "Hurry. We're going over to Uncle Denny's for dinner." I hate Uncle Denny's house and he is not a real uncle anyway. Besides, the house reeks of old cat litter and stale socks. When you drag other people to places they don't want to go it's called kidnapping. It's in the dictionary. It's illegal too. Tilda says it's because they used to steal kids when they were napping but I'm too old to have naps anymore.

Meals are awful. I can't stand the sight of steamed brown rice and broccoli dinners. I never get to say what we eat. And if I say, "Oh, not again," it's even worse. "Nothing left on the plate, please. I only wish my mother had cared what I put in my mouth when I was your age, Mara; all I ate were hotdogs I needed to heat myself."

I could live on chips and wieners.

Every night Mom asks me if I want to go for a walk by the river, sometimes with her, sometimes with her and Kurt. I hate walking. But without a TV in our home staying alone is ten times worse than putting up with her and Kurt walking hand in hand. Wink. Wink. Kiss. Kiss. Great choice. Choice should be between something I like and something I don't. Like picking between ketchup chips and plain chips. Walking or staying home alone aren't choices. Never what I want like going to Disneyland. And I'm not allowed to complain, ever. I need to complain about my mean teacher making me do extra math homework, about one chocolate bar a week, about not wearing black ever. Never allowed to shake off frustrations, shake off the stinging feeling scratching my chest.

Like the way she comes home from school, picks up the phone, and lays her problems on Carol, "You can't believe this professor. She told us the best thing that ever happened to America was Columbus . . ." I couldn't care less. But I can't tell my mother to shut up while I do my math homework. She should know what it's like depending on others, especially when she has to check the mailbox three times a day and there's nothing there. She hates it that Dad's cheques are months late.

o

Staring at the closet mirror, I'm finding parts of my mother in my face and twirling the phone cord around my wrist, listening to her carry on about how demanding I was as a child.

Of course I remember Mrs. Polanski; I just don't want to talk about her with my mother.

Mrs. Polanski was my saviour. An old widow suffering from arthritis, no children of her own. I cleaned her place every Saturday and she followed me from room to room while I dusted porcelain dolls or scrubbed the kitchen tiles on hands and knees. She offered me a shower after the housework and we took the bus together for her to buy me new clothes at Zellers. She asked about my life, my school, and my friends. I liked telling her about sneaking into bars at night, shoplifting records, because it made my life sound exciting and worth living. I remember her coarse, accented voice saying, "You young ones live quite a life, I must say." I stayed for dinner and stuffed my face. It filled me up for the rest of the week. Homemade cheese perogies, fried onions, real orange juice. We chatted through dinner, and after, I waited a minute to make room for honey cake and tea. "Such a healthy appetite," Mrs. Polanski commented, pleased I never left a crumb on my plate.

Those hearty meals had to carry me through the days when I came home from school and opened the fridge to find the old yellow bottle of mustard, like a lonely sunflower in the cold, arctic landscape. Not even a slice of bread to spread it on. My mother locked in her room, in bed with the shutters down. That's where she hid when my father walked out of the apartment for another indefinite number of weeks, after one more drunken fight, pushing each other around the living room, yelling at the top of their lungs while I buried my head under a pillow.

I shut out the sound of her feeble weeping by turning up The Doors to the max and dancing away the hunger.

The steady slur of my mother's voice at the other end of the phone line had sent me daydreaming until a thud of a glass dropping on the carpet draws my attention. She begins snoring. I stay listening. I stay thinking. I let everything sink in again. I remember why I moved away and placed a mountain range between us. I remember why before Mara was born I had gone years without talking to her. What I can't remember is why I even called her in the first place.

o

Last weekend I came home from school and, exhausted, I tripped on storage containers and sleeping bags scattered on the kitchen floor.

"We're going camping in the Rockies for the holiday weekend," my mother told me, an hour before we were leaving. I hate the swaying and the dead air in the car. I barf after the first swerve overtaking a truck. Guaranteed. And was I consulted about it? No. "It will give us some time together," my mother said, making excuses. "Is Kurt going?" I demanded with my arms crossed over my chest. "Of course, honey," she said with a goofy grin. "Besides, I have to get out of the city and away from school before I go beastly." I glared at her and threw up before we even made it to the highway.

It's not easy running away from home. I don't really want to. Besides home, the only place I know well is my school. I've been paying attention to the streets where she turns when she drives me to school. It takes twenty minutes when she's lucky and gets green lights the whole way, which is almost never. I'll hide under the school entrance's flight of concrete stairs and sneak to classes as usual in the morning. I'm running away, but I'm not stupid. I need an education.

o

Maybe I should have taken her to Disneyland. Her friends have been there at least once. I'll take her as soon as she's back. If that's what she wants, if that's what's upsetting her, if it makes her happy. I'll find the money somehow, maybe I'll ask Kurt if he will lend me the money until the custody court enforces her father's delinquent payments.

The house is a mess. I'm not talking smudges around the light switches or dust on the light bulbs. I've given up on details. I'm talking about the pile of dirty dishes in the sink. Not a single clean dish in sight, not a single fork.

I have to stop dialling Kurt's number. Now. It rings, rings, rings. Maybe he is out looking for her. On the other hand he might have gotten cold feet with this baptism of fire on the eve of moving in. As my mother said, "Kids have a knack for putting the kibosh on a new relationship." Maybe it's better this way. I can stand on my own two feet anyway. I have done it since I was thirteen.

It's true I have been a little distracted lately with exams and this new relationship giving me a taste of security again. Being held, being loved, being cherished, heck, having a life of my own — it's not a crime, is it?

o

I'm hungry and I'm going to sit on this red bench. My sling bag weighs a ton and my shoulder hurts. I don't remember what all I packed in it. I was crying. But I've got three apples, the kind I like best. Red but not the spotted red kind. I giggle at the snapping of an apple when my teeth bite into it. I also grabbed a picture of my mother just in case I'm gone for a long time. I don't want to forget what she looks like even if she isn't my real mother. I've got my Swiss Army knife in my jeans pocket in case you attack me. If it gets cold it's good to help start fires with, too. Kurt showed me how on the camping trip. The knife is tied to my belt loop so I won't lose it. I also brought a flashlight and the whole six-book collection of *Anne of Green Gables*. I can read as late as I want tonight and no one will yell, "Lights out." I also brought the multivitamins because I don't want Mom to get mad at me and Mr. Carrot for going too long without taking any. I forgot the dental floss. I hope she doesn't notice. From the corner of my eye I follow your stroll in the park until you sit on the bench across from me and unfold the newspaper, hiding your face, pretending interest in the news. You flip the pages too fast, the way I flip a story Mrs. Peterson assigns for homework. I'm not afraid because I see lots of people around and I've got my Swiss Army knife.

o

It's impossible to compete with her dad. He blows in and out of this city, unpredictable as the Chinook wind. Don't know when, or how long he'll stick around. It's always warm news for Mara. I guess for me too, in a way. It gives me a break. It's kind of a holiday for Mara. Every wish comes true, the Nintendo, the Phaser, Rollerblades, a new bicycle, a hamster. It's a great time all around, a temporary playmate. The problem shows up after, when the slushy mess is left behind and we both return to the realities of winter. What he does isn't parenting. Parenting means getting up in the middle of the night when she's sick, and so am I, but she comes first. It's telling her "no" when she's begging for candy, explaining why, and she doesn't hear, understand, or care about my reasons, saying "no" again and again and again, tempted to say "yes," to end both agonies. She cries and later in bed I cry and I don't know what to do, wondering if I'm doing the right thing and why it's so difficult, and wishing for someone lying next to me to hold me, to give me a break, a reality check, make the decisions, say the "noes," and not wanting to feel like I'll break down. And other days I say "yes" but now she knows I'll say it and she tortures me next time until I say "yes, yes, yes" to give my nerves a rest.

Parenting means cooking her favourite spaghetti pesto when I'd rather have a cheese perogy dinner cooked up for me after a whole day of classes; it's holding her in my arms when I'm fed up with it all and a part of me wishes to be thousands of miles away, sipping a margarita on a Mexican beach, and knowing I can't.

o

I ran into the kitchen yesterday to tell Mom about the new hockey card I just traded, and there she stood wrapped in her new boyfriend. They were grinning ear to ear. "We've got a surprise for you. Guess what?" I was hoping for a trip to Disneyland when she said, "Kurt is moving in. Isn't that great?" Wine glasses in hand and roses on the table. I had nothing to celebrate. No one asked my opinion. My real mother wouldn't do such a thing. She'd been away from home a lot in the last few weeks, trips here and there, weekends at the Chateau in Lake Louise, no time to play with me and shipping me to sleepovers with her no fun, prehistoric friend Carol. But that's not really the worst part. It would have been a yawn to hang around those two while they smiled like dummies into each other's eyes. The worst part is not being able to curl up with Mom in bed anymore. Since they started dating last month, on some nights the door to her room is shut and she freaks out if I walk in without knocking, the way I used to. Would my real mother ever do something like that? He can sleep with her, why can't I? They think I don't know what's going on. It sounds like those people jogging at lunch hour, out of breath.

o

Yesterday, I forced Mara to wear the beautiful green skirt her other grandmother sent for her birthday. Mara said she would rather die. If I allowed, she would wear rags, torn clothes like Ani DiFranco. She thinks I force her to wear nice clothes just to torture her. My daughter isn't about to look like a street kid. I don't want people thinking I'm an incompetent mother. That I can't keep her clean or in decent clothes. Our fridge is full, can hardly close the door. Not a chance she'll get away without a wash and scrub before the court's social work interviews. I don't want to be accused of negligence. I can handle raising a child on my own. What am I supposed to do when she refuses to wear skirts or wears the same clothes for a week?

o

I'm hiding behind a tree in the playground because I see Tilda, walking hand in hand with her parents to the see-saw. With each step, Tilda's parents lift her by the arms, swinging her in giant frog leaps. It looks fun. Like a real family. She's lucky she likes her parents, even if they're not her real parents. I hate mine. Every week arguing and slamming the phone down on each other. My father tells me my mother's a slut. My mother says he's deranged. I was a baby when they split so I don't remember ever snuggling up to them when we were living together. And now she will sleep with her new boyfriend. No use begging the fairy godmother to cast a spell on my parents so they are nice to each other again, let alone kiss and make up. I'm not Cinderella. They must have kissed once. That's how things start. Babies come after a lot of kissing. My mother and her new boyfriend kiss everywhere.

I hate Kurt even though he hasn't done anything wrong. Yet. My best friend Tilda thinks he's all right because he makes her laugh and lets her win at dominoes. I know he's going to leave like every other boyfriend has.

It's taking longer to run away than I thought. Already it's getting dark. Cars are faster than legs in getting to school. I'm tired. I'll sleep in this playground. I see you stand up from the bench and come in my direction. But I'm ready to run. You change your mind, walk toward Sammy's corner store and turn around to look at me.

I'm going to run and hide under the bushes, you'll never find me. I can't remember my way to school in the dark. If I wake up early enough I'll walk to school in the morning.

It's cold. I'll put my comfort blanket on the grass and lie down with Mr. Carrot. I'll read to him about the day Anne arrives at Green Gables.

I can't stop shivering. I hear my mother's voice calling me. Then not. I must be dreaming. I wish I was home. It was warmer hiding under the couch.

I'm dreaming strong giant arms lift me into the air. A warm white cloud carries me. The kisses are salamander wet and salty. I open my eyes and you're standing next to my mother, with the newspaper under your arm. My mother holds me too tightly, her boyfriend checks my forehead for a fever.

"Come treasure, you'll need a cosy bed and warm skin to thaw your frozen bones," she says.

I want to be mad and punch her chest. Tell her I'll never go back home but I'm so happy to see her. I missed her skin, smooth and warm, smelling of coconut cookies. She's crying.

I bite my lip but it doesn't help, I cry too. I wipe my eyes with the corner of my comfort blanket and I beg my mother to walk me home in frog leaps. "We'll need two people for that, sweets," my mother says and Kurt offers me his hand. I look at him with my best frown and wait a little. Well, maybe this one time I'll let him hold my hand. But only this one time.

I'm in the air, swinging.

KISS BABY

Willow sits April on the ground facing a small block of wood, her play dresser. On top, she balances the base of a broken bottle that reflects the feeble rays of the sun.

"No white bread either, it's no good for you." Willow brushes dirt off April's sleeve.

"But I love white bread sooo muuuuch!"

"Now, now April, do you remember Grandma Crystal being rushed to hospital? We even thought we might not see her again! And do you remember the scolding doctor? That's right . . . the doctor warned that white flour terrorized her fibre. You'd hate to waste the rest of your life in hospitals, wouldn't you?" Willow glares, arms crossed over her chest, foot tapping the ground, nodding the way adults nod when they discuss very serious matters.

"Why can't we be like everyone else and eat pizza? Why?"

o

"Orion! You scared me sneaking up like that."

"Wanna play buying candy at the mall?"

"We aren't allowed to have candy. Besides, I'm busy." Willow combs April's orange yarn strands and decides on a ponytail.

"Don't be silly. It's only pretend. You're such a baby, Sillow Willow!" Orion slides his hands into his pockets and tugs his pants further down on his hips, the way he sees older kids do.

"Stop calling me Sillow Willow! Go play your dumb candy game by yourself. It's rude to interrupt my conversation with April. Besides, April's late for school and we haven't finished her hair!" Willow decides against a ponytail and weaves April's orange strands into a braid.

"What a neat find, the broken glass!"

"That's not broken glass, it's April's mirror. Leave us alone." Orion kicks at pebbles, intending to stay.

"Just wanna look. That's all." He reaches for the glass.

"If I were you I wouldn't do that," warns Willow.

"If you were me you would be doing just that," he taunts.

o

"Don't you dare run to Mom and blame me. It was an accident! It's your fault. You shouldn't be playing with broken glass, anyway." Orion kicks April's head, setting off a nasal

and high-pitched recording: "Kiss baby. Kiss baby. Kiss baby."
Willow picks up her doll, tucks her under her arm, and runs
along the edge of the onion patch, tears streaming down her
face, one hand squeezing an injured finger, yet unable to prevent blood from dripping and staining the cuffs of her blouse.
Willow wishes she hadn't wrestled Orion: only a finger apart
in age, but so much bigger. It isn't fair, she thinks. Every time
she finds something new to play with, Orion wrestles it away.

o

"Thank you Universe, for the food on this table and bless us all.
Amen." Without delay, Fred serves himself a plate full of rice.

"Will you pass the spinach, please," yells grandmother Crystal. The yelling means she's switched off her hearing aid to
block out the commotion at mealtimes.

"Brown rice, please. Why am I always last?" complains
Willow, hugging April and concealing her bandaged finger
under the doll's long white dress. She asks her mother also
to pass the bread.

"No, Willow!" her mother says, plunking the rice in front
of her. "Stop asking questions you already know the answer
to. Do I need to repeat it daily? You are only allowed one slice
at breakfast, that's it! You know bread isn't good for you."

Those *Alive* magazines again. Willow rolls her eyes. Every
month the glossy issue feeds her mother all the latest ideas
about what is terribly good and terribly bad for her to eat.
Sometimes what is supposed to be good turns out later to be
bad, but never the other way around. She once tried to hide
the magazine in the paper box by the wood stove but Orion
told on her.

"But Mom. No fair. I like it sooo muuuuch!"

"No buts please, eat your rice now," Fred tells her with his mouth so full, some rice manages to escape and land on his lap.

"Just asking," Willow whispers. She turns her attention to building rice pyramids on her plate and offers a mouthful to April, sitting on her lap.

Her mother thinks she can fool her about health rules, but Willow knows better. Willow sometimes smells chocolate on her mother's breath during visualization and before being kissed good night. Willow and Orion are supposed to picture a bright ball of light entering their heads, travelling through their chakras, twirling in their chests, down their limbs, purifying their spirits and bodies. It's like those giant brushes twirling and spinning over the car at the car wash, leaving everything clean and shiny. Visualizations feel best for Willow on the days she catches the chocolate breath on her mother. She pictures an enormous chocolate ball, entering her mouth and melting streams of sticky sweetness along her chakras, triggering a shudder of joy. Willow's mother whispers to Fred, "Watch her body tremble. It's having a powerful effect on her."

"Don't complain, young lady. Look at your brother Orion. The poor boy is allergic to a carousel of things. Do you see him complain? He's so sensitive to everything, it's a miracle there's any food he can eat!"

"Mom, I can't eat butter, right? What's everything else I can't eat again?" Orion opens his eyes wide and tilts his head with a rehearsed innocent gaze.

"You can't have peanut butter, ice cream, cheese, or any sweets. I know it's terrible and harsh on you honey, they were your favourites." Mother ruffles his hair and smiles at him with her best eyes.

Fred adds, "Elbows off the table, Orion. And be quiet. I would hate to resort to the long stick." Since returning from an important meeting in the city on a drafty Wednesday last month, Fred caught a bad temper and has been in a foul mood. He only speaks when annoyed. Willow has also noticed that Fred has been even more agitated since the people in fancy suits started showing up around the farm last week. When they first drove up the dirt road her mother had yelled, "The bank's here," and Fred had slouched and shuffled his way to the yard to greet them, his smile forced.

Fred is tall. Willow gets dizzy when he takes her for a ride on his shoulders, pretending to be a wild horse and Willow an Amazon woman. Luckily that doesn't happen very often and even less lately. But this week, his eyes fixed on the dirt at his feet, he shrank next to the grey suits while they pointed at machinery and signed papers. As soon as they returned to their polished cars, Grandma rushed to her trailer: "Gotta dust off the service china." And Willow's mother: "Gotta water those tomatoes before they wilt on me." Even the flies vanished. Fred stomped to the wood shack and split the logs in clean sweeps. It looked as easy as slicing soft butter. Willow overheard Fred tell her mother that they couldn't afford the payments and if they don't sell land they'll have to move back to the city. She replied, "I grew up here, my parents grew up here, and I won't be selling an inch."

"Willow honey," her mother chides, "will you please sit straight. It's very important to have your back aligned with the earth." Her mother slams the salad bowl next to her. "Have some salad then."

Willow sighs. She straightens April's back, sits her between her legs. When will she grow as old as grandmother Crystal, stooped over her plate, indifferent to everything? Old enough not to be bothered by anyone. Willow finally obeys, straightens her own back.

She senses tonight isn't a great time to ask about Anita's sleepover birthday. She has been waiting for the perfect opportunity, a day when her mother laughs at Orion's jokes and swings her long hair back, eyes sparkling. This isn't the day. She senses her mother's mood by the way she slammed the salad bowl on the table. Her mother never raises her voice like other mothers.

Even though Anita's mom yells at her, Anita can do anything she wants around her house. Anita says she just needs to sob deep and long, and if she makes it look real, she gets anything she wants. Parents want to think their children are happy, in particular on a birthday. Willow has tried it on her mother. It never works and usually ends with Fred sending her to her room. Anita is lucky not to have a dad around.

The kids will be cooking their own pizzas for Anita's birthday. Willow licks her lips. She isn't planning to tell her mother that part. Her mother doesn't like her to visit Anita: she says that everything they eat at Anita's house is "sugar, salt, and grease," and apart from the junk food, their energy fields don't jive. Willow doesn't understand much about energy fields except when she wants to sit on her mother's lap and sometimes isn't allowed. "It messes Mom's aura," Willow confides to Anita.

Anita tells a different story about their mothers not jiving. She whispers that ever since they left the church, Willow's mom doesn't like hers. When Willow's mom left her dad, when Willow was still a baby, the church said she couldn't have any more bread and wine. She had to leave. Willow suspects this is the reason for her mother's weirdness about bread. But Anita's mother eats bread and as much pizza as she wants, even after they didn't allow her back in that church either.

o

"Orion, I have been meaning to ask you since we sat down why your T-shirt is inside-out. That's inappropriate at the dinner table." Fred wipes his mouth on his sleeve. He is a fly on the wall, small eyes in perpetual rotation noticing everything, catching anyone who breaks his rules.

"It's all right dear," interrupts their mother. "They had Backwards Day at school, that's all."

"Backwards Day? The world's insane. We should put them to useful work on the farm so they learn about real life."

"It's only a T-shirt, dear, harmless fun. Orion didn't mean to be rude."

Willow thinks it's a good thing Fred doesn't know Backwards Day means more than just a T-shirt. They played all day in school and during recess they went in for a quick grammar lesson. Willow isn't about to say anything because she knows when it's best to keep her mouth shut. She giggles to April. As far as she's concerned she wishes Backwards Day was every day. In her sleep, she often grows into her parents' size and they shrink into hers. She wins every argument when she grows that tall. Her reasons fall on her parents from that height the way stones fall on potato beetles, flattening them quiet.

Willow takes the opportunity of the adult eyes being focused on her brother to reach for a slice of bread sitting next to Fred.

"What's that Band-Aid doing on your finger, Willow?" Fred seems to have eyes on the back of his elbows.

"Willow told me the cat scratched her again. We must do something about that cat of yours, Fred," says her mother in the I-never-liked-your-cat-and-I'm-gonna-use-the-cat-to-scratch-you tone.

"Willow is lying again, Willow is lying again," Orion sings in delight. Willow hears Fred's breath picking up the way the wind picks up before a hailstorm.

"Did the cat scratch you, Willow?" asks Fred.

"Well no, but . . ." Willow sees his blazing eyes through the mist in her own. Her legs squeeze April.

"Did you lie, Willow? Lying is a very ugly thing."

She couldn't tell the truth. Whenever she tells on Orion, he twists her hand so mean, she must beg on her knees for mercy. Then, sometimes he stops. Her arm hurts for a long time after.

"No more bread for the rest of the week, Willow."

Her mother, furious she has used clawless words to scratch Fred, lectures Willow on the evils of lying. Willow doesn't understand how bread relates to lying and waits for the end of the lecture. It's always best not to interrupt, just bear the weight of words until there's silence again. Just the way Fred likes it.

o

"All done. I'm going to play outside now." Willow pushes herself away from the table and clasps April by the arm.

"Ah! The spinach is untouched, you're far from finished, young lady," Fred reminds her.

"Mom, you know I hate spinach. No fair."

"You aren't going anywhere until your plate is clean." Through her mother's tight stare Willow can barely see the blue in her eyes.

"But Mom, no fair. Yesterday, you didn't touch the green peppers Grandma cooked!"

"What do green peppers have to do with spinach! Lots of iron in spinach. It's good for your blood."

"But I don't wanna have green blood!"

"Don't get smart with me."

"All right, I'll feed it to April then."

"Don't play funny games with us." Fred slaps the edge of the table, making the glasses jump and a few drops of apple juice spill on the bare wood.

"No fair! No fair!" Willow drops her head between her hands.

"Would you like some cheese with your whine, princess?" Fred tosses his head back in a laugh. Willow doesn't see anything worth laughing at. Unlucky for her, this isn't one of the times he ends up laughing so hard that he chokes on his food, spraying it across the table and needing the rest of the meal to recover his breath. She hopes next time the two men in fancy suits will stuff Fred's mouth with the reams of paper in their briefcases.

"I don't want to hear another sound until that plate shines so clean you can see your reflection," says her mother.

Meanwhile, Orion seizes the opportunity to flick his brown rice off his plate and under the table where Max devours it even before it reaches the floor. Orion crosses his eyes and smirks at her. No use telling on Orion or Max. They would look offended at the allegations, their large cocker spaniel eyes as innocent as a saint's. Willow would be accused of lying again.

Orion exchanges a smile with his accomplice under the table. With all her strength, clenching her teeth, she swings her leg at Orion's knees. Misses. Max yelps.

It isn't fair. Max hates spinach. She wishes she could make spinach disappear with Max magic. Lucky Orion. She tried to feed Max once but ended up in trouble when her mother went to sweep the floor and found the mess. Meanwhile April never shows an appetite.

"No fair! No fair!" Willow turns supplicating eyes toward her grandmother and grasps her arm.

Her grandmother is nice to her. Sometimes, when Willow walks over to her trailer, Grandmother Crystal makes her toast on very white bread. Not just plain, either, but thick with strawberry jam that drips onto Willow's fingers with each bite. It's their secret. Her mother would faint if she ever found out. Grandmother is kind, the kind of person who would never hurt a fly. Not like Fred, who gets annoyed by flies bumping against the window. He likes silence when he's reading, so he stuns them with the swatter. Orion doesn't waste a second and pulls their wings off before they get back on their feet. Fred laughs, "Yeah, teach them a lesson, Orion, just to see how they'll manage now." Sometimes Orion only pulls one wing off and watches the flies spin around and around in a daze. Grandmother and Mother shudder. Bad karma, they say. They would never touch a fly, they hate blood. They bring the vacuum out to suck them up. Willow wonders if plucking wings off a fly is like having your own arm pulled off. Like those old men parading in the fall with poppies on their lapels, missing limbs. She wonders if they lost them the same way. Someone like Orion plucked their limbs off because he was annoyed at the world. She is certain those wings will never grow back; limbs never do.

o

"No, no, no fair."

Willow shakes her grandmother's arm until she fumbles with her hearing aid and listens to Willow's plea. Grandmother Crystal nods and smiles.

"You take after your mother, it must be in the blood. She was fussy with food, too."

"I bet you never forced her to eat something she didn't want to," Willow says, hopeful. She can't imagine her frail grandmother forcing anything on anyone.

"Oh yes, I remember lots of nights when she sat alone staring at a plate of green peppers, stubborn as a cabbage. Everyone else long in bed. She screamed for Tilpee, her stuffed giraffe, and eventually fell asleep with her face planted in the green peppers. The next day I would reheat the green peppers and we would begin the contest all over again."

Willow turns away from her grandmother and gazes at the horses in the pasture chewing grass. Willow already knows the first thing she'll do when she leaves home. She'll stop at the grocery store, buy the bushiest bunch of spinach and wash it with great care, cleaning the dirt trapped in the stems. Then she'll stuff her face with a loaf of white bread, as white as possible, a whole pound of butter smeared on it and maybe even chocolate. The spinach she'll dump, untouched, in the trash.

o

Willow pinches her nose and, trying to imagine chocolate, chews the spinach into a mush ball, hiding it under her tongue. She holds back her tears because tears only make matters worse. Whenever she cries Fred says, "Stop crying over nothing or I'll give you something to cry about," and swings his hand in the air as though swatting flies. "Quit your whining."

Willow excuses herself, grabs April by a leg and runs to the poplar grove behind the house to spit out the green mush under her tongue. The doll's head bouncing against her leg triggers the cries, "Kiss baby. Kiss baby."

"Shut up! Shut up!" Willow hurls the doll to the ground, and her gumboots send April flying to the creek's edge. Tears in her eyes, lips clenched, Willow runs to her doll teetering at the edge of the rushing water. She stands over the doll and spits the last of the spinach mush into the current before she raises a large stone and, with a repeated swing of her arm, crushes her doll's head.

VIVALDI'S SPRING

The phone rings and the wall-sized screen lights up.

"Hi Serena! You look fantastic. I must apologize, I won't be able to join you. You know, last-minute transmogrify to Orpheus. When are you expecting?"

"Any moment now." A radiant smile dresses the expectant mother's face. The room, decorated in clouds and filled with hovering pink ribbons and balloons, bubbles with festivity.

Cristiana blows Serena a goodbye kiss while projecting a 3-D stork into the room. Higher up a few balloons pop. The room bursts into laughter. Champagne flutes sweep in mid-air and converge with a clink. Good auspices. Vivaldi's Spring Concerto plays in the background.

In the yard, the roar of the men playing soccer erupts and climbs through the window left ajar. Tess, pressing her hand to the sill, observes the celebration after a goal is scored. The men leap in joy and bump fists. A little too loud, a little too long, a show of bravado to cover up their impatience with the slow delivery. After the goal they look up. Not at the window. Not at her. Further up in the firmament, perhaps at the invisible Goddess that led the ball inside the posts.

Tess returns her attention to the birth room. She exchanges a meagre, polite smile with Serena and remains outside the circle of excitement that surrounds the mother. The grandmother, in her twenties, steps forward and deposits a pinkish package on the future mother's lap. She sits beside Serena. In this long-awaited moment, the grandmother will reveal the child's name, a name it is said the grandmothers receive while under galactic trance, and that they then tenderly embroider on sweaters they pattern themselves. Serena accepts the gift and places the envelope containing the birth expenses and the service fee on the grandmother's lap. They exchange light kisses and the bluegenta smudge of colour sticks to each cheek.

Tess fixes her gaze on the package. The women seem to have forgotten its existence and carry on with their conversations. Excitement builds as they share stories of their own birth experiences, the months of anxiety to decide on the myriad of available choices for birthing. Tess, unable to contain her curiosity, reaches over Serena's shoulder and tears the wrapping paper. The violin's melody saturates the room in the abrupt silence following the gasps of disbelief and the covered mouths. Tess states the given name embroidered on the sweater, clenches the hand holding the package. She should have not confided her favourite girl's name to Serena when as children they played at motherhood.

Serena throws an ivy glare at Tess and is about to say something when Tess discreetly taps her own left wrist with the index finger of her other hand and smiles.

After the hint of a frown perceived only by Tess, Serena exclaims without missing a social beat: "Inina! It's so unusual! Fantastic."

Everyone sighs and claps.

Champagne flutes rise again and one by one the women reveal their pleasant wishes for the child's future, a nightingale's voice to enchant, a smile to endear, the gift to grow up a leader as befitting of her parents' indigo tattoo status.

Shoulders deflated, Tess's fingers mindlessly drum on the cuff of her blue blouse, which conceals the purple tattoo on her wrist. The cuff is Miguel's invention. It conceals an electronic scrambler that dampens the tattoo's signal to the social un-networking alarm radars intended to prevent people from trespassing social networks established by birth. The Celtic ribbon pattern she should leave visible at all times distinguishes her as one of the people who still work. Who cannot afford designer babies and their copywritten birth names.

o

Tess ponders her options. Her motherhood licence expires in forty-eight hours, on her twentieth birthday. A policy intended to offer citizens the illusion of choice, for of course she has not had sufficient time to save up for her dream child. Not to mention that Miguel insists he is not carved for children. In the past, to keep the matter out of sight, out of feeling, she even refused to watch the popular birth shows of the movie stars. Yesterday, Miguel, in his thrill-of-the-forbidden nightly hacks into the Network, convinced her to crash Serena's intimate birth party, curious to peek at this rare and privileged ritual announced on the exclusive social glamour networks. Tess had numbed out the matter of children, until she showed up unannounced at her childhood best friend's event. Miguel, anticipating her hemorrhage of emotions, slipped an anti-anxiety pill into her purse when they left the house to catch the solar hovercraft to the party.

Tess snaps off a thornless rose from the hydroponic vase as she returns to the window. Miguel moves down the field with the finesse of a rhythmic gymnast in control of the ball. Tess twirls the flower beneath her nostrils. There is no scent. She smirks at this expensive, genetically altered variety for allergy sufferers. Serena, who could barely afford a plastic rose from the dispense machine, is now, thanks to the skin counterfeiters, married into another tattoo colour. Having eschewed her past, she now only needs to worry about what tint of hair will match her hourly outfit adjustments. Miguel dribbles past a player and races toward the goal. A few paces from the goalkeeper he swings his leg to strike an assured shot. A defenceman, in a last frantic effort, hooks Miguel's foot from behind and he collapses onto the grass. The thud echoes across the yard and sparks an outraged shriek from his teammates. Tempers flare. Tess shakes her head, unable to comprehend a game that in a matter of seconds elicits more passion in her man than an entire year sharing their home life. She thought nothing would squeeze an emotion out of him until this moment. Miguel gesticulates and moves with renewed energy and purpose as he argues with the guilty player. Could those gloved hands toss and catch a newborn in the air with the same assurance they handle a ball in a throw-in? Tess does not recognize those same hands now so alive in the field, hands that seemed lost and hidden behind his back anytime she suggested a child to bring a curveball to their already predictable married life of six years.

o

Tess turns her back on the men's game in the yard just as they end the play and gather around the barbecue. Serena basks in the motherhood glow of her self-inflating maternity dress. The remote-controlled crib, the atomic-powered rocking horse, the wardrobe of tiny endearing garments awaken Tess's maternal instincts. She reaches for her carbonytrate purse to check the amount of unused credits in her bank account. Hesitates. Even the 24-hour discount outlets with high perishable ratios have been at the limit of her dreams. The cost of delivery and the grandmother would send her over the top. She sighs a little too loud and the women turn toward her with a quizzical smile. She decides not to open the purse.

The video-phone rings again.

"Congratulations Serena, your contractions have just begun." Dr. Hoffman appears on the wall-screen, a chart in his hand, reading glasses a sneeze away from slipping off the tip of his nose. The room erupts. More balloons and champagne bottles pop. Pink paper streamers shoot through the air. Serena struggles to contain joyous tears.

"How long would you like the labour to last?"

Speechless, Serena grins at the doctor. Her scintillating teeth highlight her smile. With a coy shrug that brings her pendular gold earrings to touch her shoulders, she turns her smile around the room, seeking guidance from the breathless women also expectant for her answer. The grandmother, cool-headed on these occasions, steps forward and asks those present if an hour suits everyone. She receives cheers for an answer.

"An hour will be just fine, Dr. Hoffman," the grandmother says with a knowing wink.

Everyone gathers in a crescent moon around the screen. Serena and the grandmother sit at the front. They sink with a sigh of comfort into the embroidered cushions from ancient India depicting Ganesh in a myriad of tantric positions. The grandmother holds the future mother's hand. A woman sitting behind Serena massages her shoulders. The grandmother activates the preprogrammed scent diffuser on the wall-screen and the perfume of lilies wafts through the room.

Tess returns to the window. Bored and restless, the men in the controlled-environment yard toss a Frisbee and take urgent swigs from the bottles in their free hands. A few intermittent words, followed by a laugh, interrupt their restless silence. The number of empties scattered around the yard tells Tess that the men have waited too long to finally see the baby for the first time. Now and then they pause to glance up at the window. There is nothing else to do. They await the annunciation. Nuno, the father, stands by the barbecue, oiling and re-oiling the grasshoppers in a peppercorn marinade. She waves to Miguel and walks back to join the women. The image on the screen focuses on the baby, who stirs in a Plexiglas case. Clear plastic tubes attach to the bottom of the case and disappear from view. Vivaldi's flute lends its calm aura to the room. The baby's tiny hands curl in a fist. Serena holds the camera's remote control and zooms in on the face. Eyelids and mouth closed, the baby begins to turn. Her wonderful and perfect feet kick in slow motion. The seconds tick at leisure in the face of a new life being born.

The baby's toes wriggle. Collective chuckles of pleasure follow. Tess decides to surprise Miguel. Tomorrow she will stop by the cash-and-carry Morning Star birth clinic and pick up a baby on her way home. She will charge it to her credit card even if that means they both will have to work ten extra hours a week for ten years at the spare ribs lab farm. On the other hand she might be able to press Serena for a free loan, considering they are the only survivors of the dismantled no-clones student resistance movement of their youth and Tess is the only person who knows Serena's secret past.

o

Dr. Hoffman's voice returns.

"So, what do you think?"

"A work of art, Doctor. The picture I had envisioned." Serena claps with the tips of her fingers and makes no noise. After she wipes a tear collecting at the edge of the eye, she rests her hands over her heart. In unison the room stops breathing.

The baby girl already shows the first strands of black hair on her head. Her nose alludes to Greek perfection, her skin to Scandinavian paleness, with the option to tan, her lips thin and tiny reflect Serena's only concession to this year's fashion. She did not wish to produce a misfit child, teased for the rest of her life by same-year peers. The baby does not resemble either parent, an advantage in adolescence when she will want to avoid public affinity with her embarrassing progenitors. Serena confides to the grandmother in a way that allows everyone in the room to hear, "I paid a fortune for the state-of-the-art chromosome manipulation to generate true blue blood. Everything I had fantasized for myself."

Tess knows she cannot expect much from a last-minute motherhood impulse. Only a modest trait selection is available through the twenty-four hour discount outlets. She will cherish the less-than-perfect child, rejected by disillusioned, wealthy parents faced with the reality of unplanned designer incompatibilities or displeased with the mangled aesthetic results.

She will avoid the school of genetics' outlet and their artsy aberrations, experiments with fringe aesthetic theories: multi-shaded eyes, asymmetrical ears, a nose hanging from a chin or, Venus help her, from an even less expected place. She admits her fondness for the race mosaics passing on the streets: Nordic hair with African skin and Asian eyes. Exotic and in good taste. A celebration of humanity.

o

At the sixty-minute mark a beep signals the imminent birth. Serena's hand trembles.

Dr. Hoffman's voice returns with the deep resonance of a tenor leading a celestial symphony.

"Come on, Serena, you can do it. The big moment has arrived. You cannot falter now. Push. Push."

With rehearsed tenderness, the grandmother kisses Serena's forehead and helps her point the remote control at the Plexiglas. Serena, revealing stress in her clenched jaw, wavers. Her hand droops under the invisible and heavy moment that will transform the rest of her life. For a moment she appears to hesitate. The grandmother reminds Serena to concentrate on her breathing, to mimic her own exaggerated and laboured inhalations and exhalations. Serena relaxes after a few breaths and with the burden of anticipation at last pushes the button on the remote.

A gong resonates throughout the room. On the monitor, a gigantic hammer swings, cracks the Plexiglas case. The brine water solution breaks and spills in a torrent. The whoosh of the water propels the baby down a spiral slide and she lands on a gelatin-cushioned bassinet. The newborn cries.

Tess will not relinquish such an important moment in the birth experience. She detests the impersonal and dehumanizing probes of technology. The hammer, she will swing herself. And after the waters break she will pick up the child from the strainer-bassinet and hold her next to her heart. Despite knowing that the baby will be sticky and mucky from the gelatin, Tess understands the baby's need to hear the mother's heartbeat for a healthy bonding experience. She does not care if her friends accuse her of behaving like an unsanitary Luddite to actually want the baby in the room with her.

o

Outside, the men, hearing the much-awaited gong, cheer. "Hip hip hooray! Hip hip hooray!" They lock in a joyous embrace and hop in a circle of hollers and hoots, members of an immemorial tribe, grateful to have abandoned the callous ancient tradition of having men present and helping during the birth show. The fireworks of bottles crashing against the wall enter the open window and fill the upstairs room. It is not long before feet hammer along the staircase and corridor, a thunder of motion approaching the room. The women look with expectation at the door. The father, leading, rushes into the room and runs to the screen. Focused on the baby's smiling face, he fills the screen with kisses. He talks to his child at a speed even adults cannot comprehend. The infant waves her hands, she attempts to grasp a non-existent breast among the new maze of tubes and needles genetically testing and immunizing her at once. Unsuccessful, she continues her protesting screams until a mechanical arm descends with a bottle of warm milk. Next, the father turns, kisses the exhausted mother and with the tail of his shirt pats the beads of sweat on the mother's brow.

The room bursts in applause. A few uncontained shrieks pierce the remaining hovering pink balloons. The jubilant father jumps to his feet, opens a four-foot champagne bottle and showers the guests with foam. The din drowns the last of Vivaldi's notes. Hypnotized by the endearing child suckling and hiccupping, Tess ignores the successive commotion of toasts in the room, and stares until the grandmother turns the screen off. The celebration will continue into the night and the following morning when everyone walks to the balmy yard, a champagne flute in hand, following the aroma of barbecued grasshoppers.

HELL'S HELL

Aluminum utensils clatter and echo in the officers' cafeteria. The men occupying the two lines of long tables on the wooden benches shout to be heard above their own din and the creaky ceiling fans. Sweat drips from their brows, their torsos glisten and not even the indefatigable blades on the ceiling fans succeed in mowing down the humidity, although they manage to keep the torture of mosquitoes and flies at bay.

"Hell's hell but the cash buys a few years of heaven back home." Luandino has acquired this annoying ability to Braille my thoughts after two years together on the front line, and he's on a roll. "Save your funeral face for the bona fide occasion, Gusto. I'm not dead yet, only quitting this Lucifer's Grill to fly home to the wife and kids. Be happy for me. I'll send you a leg of *presunto* as soon as I repurchase the farm from the bank." He swings a punch to my shoulder that's all brake and no turbo. Luandino is the only crazy monkey in this unit who signed on for a two-year stint after his compulsory conscription to crush the indigenous insurrection. "Better pay than when hoeing my rocky corn terraces," he would snort.

Luandino, the lucky bastard, is on his way out now while I'm due for more hell on my own before my front-line flying log lifts me out of here. Two years and we're the last survivors from a fresh unit of forty. First down, Major Ferreira. After a week of yelling to the rookie pilot, "Watch the frigging wires at the end of the landing pad, they'll strangle your chicken neck one day," Major Ferreira dunks five of the instructors with him in the tangle of the stupid electric snare. Go figure. In my nightmares I still hear the screams before the chopper hit the ground. The rest? Downed one by one on kamikaze missions to salvage the maimed on the front.

"Gusto, let's fly the patrol along the front line, up to the coast for a dip in the red-light district of Mukambo. It'll help wash that funeral face off." Luandino flips a small wad of payday cash next to the soup bowl, spits on his fingertips, and pats down his sideburns. "It's on me. Shall I whet your appetite a tad more, hon?" He slides next to my soup bowl a photo of us and two gals draped over the wings of a plane. He winks, cleans the inside of his soup bowl with what's left of his ring finger, shoves it in his mouth to suckle it clean. All the while he purses his lips, bats his eyes faster than a chopper's blade.

I snatch the photo and tear it in four, drop it on the floor.

"Hey, hey, afraid the missus back home gets hold of the

incrimination?" This time the punch to my shoulder is all turbo.

I growl and wave a kamikaze fly away from my soup. The cafeteria's glass wall offers a view of the hangar and rattles with the approach landing of another T-6. The men on my bench stop chewing for a glance at the smooth touchdown before carrying on with their chatter.

Luandino's the only guy with the guts to divert a reconnaissance mission over enemy territory into a safari, shooting enough antelope for an entire week's menu. We'll miss him.

"I'd feed this whey-shit to the pigs if I weren't starving. Coming on patrol or what?"

I shrug. We're due to drop off supplies and armaments to the front lines. We've survived our fair share of close calls together. The time the damn antelope came to in midflight over the Kwanza river. I sumo-wrestled the devil, sliced its throat, just before it would have brought us down for crocodile bait.

"Coming or not?"

"I'm in." A voice halfway between cockerel and rooster climbs over my right shoulder, trips over itself and lands inside the conversation.

Luandino and I stick together like bowl and spoon so the men along the rows of the long table go monk and crane their necks to check out the voice thin enough to make an annoying paper cut on the ear.

"Toino." He squeezes himself in beside me and extends his hand over my soup and Luandino's. Neither of us takes it. I inspect the ceiling, watch the flies hanging near the fan for coolness.

"Sorry, friends first. In war, don't friggin' go anywhere

without them. First piece of advice you jackpot for free, rookie."

"I volunteered to the choppers. Ain't here to watch mosquitoes buzz."

This fellow, rosy baby fat still jiggling his cheekiness, must be replacing the rookie who jumped funny out of the chopper last week before touchdown and was instantly sucked up. Nice clean cut.

"We've got an eager one here!" Luandino booms, taking in the rookie with a sideways glance.

Out of the corner of my eye I measure this sacrificial virgin who's not even intimate with a razor blade yet. We must be losing this war for headquarters to package up these officers in such a hurry, no time to muck them up in training camp with a few black eyes and barbed-wire scars that will never heal in this muggy weather.

Luandino lays it on. "You'll have plenty of time to play with mosquitoes in the hovering cradle. Sorry, it's our last buddy flight together. Sort of a date, y'know?" He teases him with a wink.

The rookie swallows his first spoonful of soup and cringes. He pushes the bowl away, shrugs his shoulders and disappears. The pack of jackals on our row, always rooting for a face pushed into the latrine or a fist bloodied, howls in laugher. Luandino shrugs, nudges the bowl over and helps himself.

"How about it, then? We spoil ourselves on the last flight?"

"Sure," I say.

He stands up and swings his hips, arms flailing above his head, pretending he's a hot stripteaser.

"An extra-long stop in Mukambo for some deserved fun!"

"Sure."

"Better hurry with your Consommé Aux Legumes or Le Chef will be offended. No tricks this time to keep me in hell with ya, buddy. I don't wanna be penalized another week on my early leave for a stupid late takeoff. Can you count to ten, Gusto?"

The head cook shuffles over, dragging his flip-flops on the greasy tiled floor. His cigarette hangs over the corner of a scarred lip and the dishtowel in his hand wipes sweat from his glistening head and neck.

"Look at this personal attention, Le Chef himself swinging by to ask his distinguished guests how everything tasted and perhaps offer us dessert. How marvellous! Crème Brûlée you said?"

"Shut up, Luandino. Urgent phone call from Commander Neves to Lieutenant Augusto," the cook says with a smirk and a light smack of the towel on Luandino's nape.

Fearing I'm getting rotten news from home, I torpedo to the phone at the far corner of the cafeteria, just outside the kitchen door.

"Ten minutes. I'll go ahead," Luandino says, stuffing the wad of cash back into his pocket.

The phone, smudged with flour and crackling static, blasts my ears. "Hello," I scream into the receiver. A voice, not Commander Neves, instructs me to glue on to the phone and await instructions for a secret mission. The Commander's on the other line with the President and I'm shut out of the conversation. The President? Something big is up with this useless colonial war. As usual I'm in the dark following orders boomeranged from I don't know where.

The constant traffic of the kitchen runner clearing the tables keeps the swinging doors opening and closing, fanning a smell of onions and garlic into the mess and slapping my face with the sticky heat of frying rancid oil. That liver-wrenching dinner preview coming from the vegetable sauna is making my trip with Luandino look better by the second. Through the window I see Luandino already in his olive flight-suit climbing into the chopper. He waves me to join him.

Damn, useless, motherfucker Commander, always bored at his desk, inventing bloody moves and dirty tricks to keep this war alive and the diamonds and gold flowing into his and the President's pocket. If it weren't for their greed I wouldn't be marinating here with the boys.

The mechanic runs in yelling.

Luandino's giving me thirty seconds to bazooka my ass to the chopper. Damn. Luandino thinks I'm pulling his leg again so he'll be late on takeoff.

"Tell him to hang on. I'm on the line to the Commander. Swear on my grave."

I wait some more. I wipe the sweat trickling down my forehead and twirl the long cord around the blue heart tattoo on my forearm.

Out of the corner of my eye I catch my personalized red flight-suit and silver helmet sprinting across the runway and into the chopper. The doors close. Motherfucker Luandino's taking off without me.

The few men left in the cafeteria break out laughing. I realize there's no Commander on the other line and smash the receiver on the tile floor. Smart-ass rookie. I shake my fist at the lifting chopper then slowly drop it into my pocket as the tail rotor whirls off through the air and the chopper spins on itself at the hands of the torque. Frigging tail rotor wasn't bolted properly. Damn dumb drunk mechanic fuckers.

The cafeteria, a graveyard of silence, stares wide-eyed as the impact of the tail rotor on the roof busts the cafeteria glass and sends everyone diving to the floor. Trickles of red run down my nose from the hail of glass shattering my face. The centrifugal force of the chopper spinning out of control spits the rookie Toino onto the ground. Then Luandino. The metal fuselage collapses.

Luandino curling up in flames, screaming, his flesh roasting. "Hell's hell . . ." his voice from minutes ago detonates in my head. Hell's not just knowing why a buddy goes up in smoke and why I'm the one left from my unit to watch it. It's wondering when I am next, maybe tomorrow or maybe next week; wondering which frigging way I will go, and praying it's brisk and merciful.

I don't want to taste the burning heat of my buddy's skin, I don't want to smell that gasoline geyser cloud, I don't want to listen to his screams till silence is king, my fists like dead rocks buried in my pockets, unable to budge a fucking finger. I stare at medics rushing into the chopper mayhem, punched back by the flames and heat as the wad of bills, now scattered, flutters in the air, over the debris, twirling and dancing above the rising flames, untouched by the bloody carnage.

IMMORTALITY

Vera rummaged in the wood crate overflowing with fluffy moss she and her brother had collected that morning in the pine woods behind her parents' riverside home. The moss's cool softness dampened her fingers. After careful inspection, she found a wide patch of greenery to cover the refuge of stacked pebbles and slate roof she had assembled on the fireplace mantle. The refuge, in reverence referred to as the Holy Cave by her mother, would shelter the clay figure of Baby Jesus in the manger, surrounded by Mary, Joseph, and the cows. Through the moss an oak seedling thrust upward, lending a realistic touch to the miniature world Vera had created. She stepped back to evaluate the effect of the green nativity scene growing over the smooth white marble of the fireplace, the hills where the shepherd with the dusty pink beret still insisted on playing the half-missing recorder, his brown-painted trousers showing more chips than trousers. From an original herd of twenty faithful surrounding the shepherd, three sheep now listened, miraculous survivors of years of dives onto the tiled kitchen floor after slipping from *rabanada*-greasy little fingers. Strangely, it still seemed that nothing had been added, nothing taken, in this nativity scene. As if no time had passed.

"Christmas isn't Christmas without the laughter and commotion of children," Mother said, her eyes anchored on the bowl where baguette slices drowned in a mixture of sugar and port before the final splash into the deep fryer. "Children bring joy to the world," she added.

"Not at all. It's headaches they bring. The parents I know act as if they can't wait for their children to grow up and leave. Many don't even pay attention to the children now, skypeing, texting, or tweeting on the phone while their kid throws a tantrum." Vera spoke in a loud, dry tone. Her father, in the rocking chair, lowered the newspaper and peered at them over his reading glasses; her brother, standing next to her, stopped unwrapping a wise man riding a camel and cleared his throat. She regretted her barbed pitch.

"I know you think we didn't do a proper job of raising you," Mother said, fetching additional cinnamon from the lower cupboard.

Vera bit her tongue and focused on placing the last patch of moss on the floor of the refuge in order for her brother to complete the Holy Cave scene.

"I didn't say that. But it's the 21st century and women can

choose whether to have kids or not. And from what I see, a lot of people should choose not to." Vera strove for melody in her words while stacking another hill of flat river stones for the castle to stand upon.

"Delfim loves children," Mother said dryly.

"Enough to quit his job in the see-saw of the sky and dedicate himself to raising them?" She lifted her eyebrows with sarcastic inflection.

"We could look after the children. And now that we are retired, we would like a little distraction. It's been terribly empty since you kids left home." Mother sighed, wiping her hands on her apron, then continued, "I'm so sorry I told you that I couldn't wait for you to leave the house. But it was so long ago."

"I'm not having children in order for you to raise them."

"All right, all right then." Mother turned the propane setting on the stovetop higher and the oil sizzled, spraying over the rim of the deep fryer. "Ouch," she said theatrically, licking the top of her hand to cool the stinging.

Tomé hummed an upbeat version of "O Holy Night" to remind everyone of the spirit of the season. The sizzling *rabanadas* perspired their cinnamon, perfuming every pore of the kitchen. This sweet and pungent scent of oil penetrated their clothes and skin and transported them to an exotic land of spices and colour; it mitigated the fustigating rain on the windowpanes, punctuated by the occasional thunder.

"When are we going to see grandchildren in this family? It isn't something you leave for retirement," Father insisted in a sharp tone from behind the newspaper, this time without bothering to surface for eye contact.

"Well Father, perhaps kids arrive the day they trust their grandfather will begin to pay attention to what they are actually saying, no?" Flustered, Vera picked up the empty wood crate and slammed it against the tile floor. Pivoting on her heels, she prepared to exit the kitchen, perhaps even the house once more in the middle of another Christmas, when she inadvertently elbowed Tomé and sent the Baby Jesus in his hand flying.

In horror, the four stared at the swift ascension of the clay figure before its even swifter descent to the tile floor where it crashed with a loud snap. Before their eyes, Baby Jesus bounced in a trinity of separate parts, severed at the head and waist.

They stood motionless, the sizzling of the oil interrupted by the occasional prolonged sigh of someone finding their breath again. Her father, steadying himself on his cane, rose from his seat in slow motion and shuffled to the base of the fireplace. He struggled to lower himself to his knees and collected the dismembered Baby Jesus in the tender weave of his fingers.

He evaluated the unexpected scene on his hand. Baby Jesus' face appeared unperturbed.

"Nothing crazy glue can't fix these days." He raised his head and smiled, to the relief of the family.

o

Standing next to the fireplace with the crackling flames as his musical accompaniment, Tomé finished his tenor rendition of "Silent Night" under the proud applause of his family.

"What a treat. A private concert by the best tenor in the country. Aren't we lucky?" Vera planted a kiss on her brother's cheek after he lifted his head from his playful and exaggerated bow.

"Well, well, you are too kind," Tomé said, showing his professional smile. "We should save the applause for Father's emergency surgery on Baby Jesus. You should consider moonlighting as a saint, healing the broken ones," he added with a light wink to his father, who was gently swaying on the rocking chair by the window with the newspaper open on his lap.

Father's eyes sought out Vera, who turned her back on him and concentrated on pinning an aluminum foil star above the Holy Cave. "Just wish it was that easy when it came to real life," her father concluded with a sigh.

Her mother cleared her throat and spoke to change the mood.

"Tomé, do you remember that first year when your father laid Baby Jesus on the moss?" Mother fished the second batch of *rabanadas* from the sweltering oil.

"Vaguely," mumbled Tomé, sprinkling threads of sawdust in convoluted pathways that led to the Holy Cave, where a deadpan Baby Jesus displayed his post-surgery scars.

Vera readjusted the aluminum star over the refuge and remembered how, as a child, she had fought with her brother Tomé for the honoured task of trail-maker. Year after year he convinced her she traced the flimsiest, most boring and predictable paths, therefore she should leave the artistic responsibility to him.

Mother's loud rambling persisted, unintelligible above the sputtering oil, and Vera, noticing the pallor of her mother's face, whispered to Tomé, "How's she doing?"

"I think the whirlwind of Christmas distracts her from the pain."

Vera turned and observed Mother busying herself around

the stove, dusting a new batch of *rabanadas* in cinnamon and sugar, her rigid body a castle of stubbornness.

"I'll never forget the fuss. You were five, Tomé," Mother continued, "and you were screaming and screaming, thinking Baby Jesus would catch pneumonia lying bare on the damp moss."

"Such a sensitive porcelain boy you were, little brother," Vera blurted in a sharp tone. Without mercy, rolling her eyes, she cut short the story Mother repeated every December, "But thank heaven Father rushed to the wood shop, carved a pine manger and glued some sprigs of straw in it. Voilà. The End. Finito. Everyone happy."

Her father, sitting by the window, following the convoluted pathways of the rain on the window pane, shrugged in quiet resignation and returned to his newspaper pages.

o

Mother polished the kitchen counter with slow, deliberate, circular motions while the family waited by the dining room entrance.

"No one's allowed to dinner before tucking their best shoe under the chimney. Baby Jesus refuses to leave presents otherwise," she said, projecting her weakened voice along the corridor with the makeshift megaphone of her open hand next to the mouth.

"And will lights still blow out before he climbs down the chimney?" Vera shook her head in exasperation. "We're not children anymore, Mother."

Tomé frowned at her, walked back to the kitchen to meet Mother.

"Must I eat dinner barefoot?" Tomé looked at her with an amused glance. "Some traditions should retire at some point, no? I don't live here anymore, nor do I travel with a spare shoe wardrobe."

"Can't argue with tradition," insisted Mother. "Who would have predicted that this boy, who used to bring out his whole shoe collection on Christmas Eve, eager to hoard presents, would turn out to be so cynical?"

"I'll fetch a pair of old slippers then, and shuffle along somehow." Tomé tossed an arm around Mother's shoulder, stealing her white tea towel from her hand. He waved the cloth at Vera, still standing by the doorway to the living room. "Come on, be a honey, get rid of those tight heels and get some comfortable slippers on. Join us in the spirit of the season, will ya?"

Vera looked at her hopeful mother and, with reluctance, returned to the kitchen. She accepted Father's old slippers, which Mother handed to her. While Tomé lined everyone's shoes in a row by the fireplace, Mother leaned closer and whispered in her ear, "You know, your father has always regretted what happened all those years ago but could never say it."

Tomé returned and teased them, "It's a tad late now to start keeping secrets in this family, isn't it?" He laughed, placed his long arms over both their shoulders and ushered them into the dining room.

o

Father faced the dining room window, his gaze wandering the inscrutable sky, pausing on the pine trees bending against the unholy wind of winter. Poised to his right, nearest the door, Mother sat within view of her kitchen at the end of the hallway.

"Guess who phoned wondering if you were home for Christmas?"

"Can't imagine," Vera said, although she guessed Clarinda, her friend from elementary school. She struggled to grip a stubborn walnut sliding from the nutcracker's jaws.

"Clarinda, dear! She just gave birth to an adorable set of twins. I told her you were coming and she said she would love to have you pay her a visit!" Mother poured five drops of olive oil over the salted cod. The collards and the boiled potato were not as fortunate.

"In my time walnuts and figs were eaten last, after the proper meal." Father spoke without removing his gaze from the outside, where the wind whistled with renewed zest and for a moment drew the room's attention.

"In your time . . . in your time! Nothing is ever what it should be and I never learn the proper ways." She spoke without rancour this time.

"Need some help?" Tomé offered his nutcracker.

"I'll manage. The struggle is half the fun." Vera clenched her teeth and half-cracked the walnut shell, digging the nut out with a fork. As a child she had called it picking brains. Back then, she squeezed the hard shell into the gap of an open door, slammed the door, and crunched the shell. Now, she sliced a dried fig and tucked the brain in.

"Tough little heads these buggers have." Father fit two nutshells inside his palm and closed his iron grip in a single loud snap. The shells shattered. "Never fails. Use like to fight like," he said, absent-minded, sorting through the shells and chewing on broken walnut chunks.

"Father, I thought walnuts weren't to be touched 'til last!" Vera said with a good-natured chuckle, slipping her slippers on and off her feet under the table.

He glanced at the half-eaten walnut in his hand, raised his eyebrows, and swallowed the rest.

o

Vera stared at her plate overflowing with boiled potatoes, collards, and a thick cod fillet. She splashed her food with a generous amount of golden olive oil. In the background, Mother's voice droned on.

"Remember the Christmas Eve Vera decided to stand guard by the fireplace to catch Baby Jesus in action filling the shoes with presents?"

For the first time that evening Vera noticed colour in Mother's cheeks, a return to the vigorous years.

"Everything was going well until Vera's bladder forced her to abandon her post. And would you believe it, as soon as Vera had walked to the washroom and sat on her potty, Baby Jesus blew out the lights and dropped the presents down the chimney." Mother sent Vera a teasing wink and her eyes sparkled. "Poor Vera, her pants locked around her legs and one hand on the potty, pressing it against her buttocks, she tried to run down the stairs and stumbled. What a disaster."

In the past, irritated by another predictable cycle of stories that seemed designed to embarrass her, Vera would have disappeared into the washroom before the end of her mother's story. This year, she controlled an old impulse and remained seated, smiling along to her family's laughs at the pee-pot story, watching her mother's face illuminated as though time had not passed, pain did not consume her.

o

Vera nibbled on a boiled potato, pushed it aside, mashed cornbread in her plate to absorb the olive sea on the bottom. Her favourite part of the meal. The salted cod scraped her throat, brought her the scent of childhood vacations by the Atlantic, a memory of the rogue wave that swept her to sea while she played in the wet sand, the salted cod an echo of that same ocean brine that flooded down her throat before her mother yanked her from the chilly water by the back of her wetsuit. Her mother's voice, even then in the background, telling her stories, calming her cries, soothing her like the rhythmical surf of every holiday year.

There were not many tales to be told of her present life. In the dark, with her purring cat on her lap, combing his grey coat with the rake of her long fingernails, she often waited for Delfim to arrive at the strangest hours, jetlagged and exhausted. He slept during daylight hours when she was eager to socialize and enjoy his brief time in the city. She touched more of their cat than of her husband and silence reigned as the prevalent music channel in her home. She wondered whether a child would indeed anchor Delfim home. He tried to assure her with his usual nose-rubbing charm, "It's not like you'd be raising the children alone. I'd be here to help." Help. Why was the woman the one to always sacrifice her career in the name of family?

Mother stood up to replace the guttering candles on the dining-room table. A dizzy spell forced her to grasp Father's chair, the other hand attempting to conceal her pallid face. With a panicked look, Father hurried from his outward gaze and awkwardly tossed his comforting hand onto Mother's.

Vera imagined a large wave, a whitecap snatching her mother's frayed and defenceless body, limbs flailing, engulfed by seaweed. Vera waist-deep in the pulling tide, without steady footing, unable to help, unable to save her mother from drifting further to sea.

Tomé and Vera rose to assist Mother. Mother waved them to sit. Before dinner, while singing grace, they had been a chain of hands, a frail link to each other, an anchor. Tomé disregarded Mother's dismissal and rushed to the kitchen to fetch another round of candles.

Vera sat down again. She poured an excessive amount of olive oil onto her plate and, swaying her fork, caused minor waves. She crumbled an encore of cornbread into the olive sea, and with her fork mashed the dough.

Vera saw Mother and Father submersed to their necks, holding hands, the link of their fingers slipping as their strength waned; Mother and Father in troubled waters, looking to the shore, reminiscing on their lives, looking for an anchor, seeing only Tomé and herself.

Mother lowered herself onto her seat and watched Tomé replace the candles. A smile lit her face again.

Vera renewed the attack on the boiled cod fillet on her plate with a stab of her fork.

o

"Everyone ready for Christmas cake?" Mother motioned with her freckled chin, preparing to stand up.

"Stay still for once, Mother. I'll fetch it," Vera said, jumping up. With affection, she pressed her mother's shoulder.

"It's sitting on the kitchen table. Don't forget dessert plates."

"I'll find my way."

"I'll give you a hand." Tomé followed as Vera walked toward the kitchen.

The ring-shaped loaf, studded with bright dried fruits, reminded Vera of rubies and emeralds, a crown of precious stones. The powdered sugar sprinkled on top gave the impression of snow dust on a hill.

"Let's see, do I still remember where the dessert plates are stored?" Tomé swung open the middle door. He found spices instead.

"Why is Mother so obsessed about grandchildren? Why me and not you? Does she know?" Vera stood on her toes and peeked into the upper cupboard shelves for the crystal cake dish.

"Bachelors are exempt from certain questions. I count on my dear sister to take care of succession duty," Tomé grinned and teased with a wink.

"Very funny."

"I'm serious." He raised his hand, mimicking a moment in court. "According to her sewing needle I'm out of the race."

"Her sewing needle?!" Vera placed her hands on her hips.

"She swears by it and claims it has never lied to her when it comes to births. And there we have it, ta-dah." Tomé wrapped one arm around Vera's shoulder.

"How do you know?"

"Happened to stumble into her 'Winds of Fate' reading last Easter."

Vera looked at him sideways, doubtful.

Tomé continued. "A long thread, with a needle dangling from the end, dipped half a dozen times over your photograph."

"My photograph?" Vera dropped a silver fork on the red tiled floor.

"Well, it's supposed to be over your right palm but I don't presume you would agree to that."

"Bloody right."

"You should have seen Mother's eyes bugging out, her hand still as hope waiting for the needle's answer."

"And the answer?"

"The answer amazed her, she couldn't believe her eyes," Tomé said, absorbed in double-checking the number of dessert plates in his hand.

"Come on, spill the beans."

"I thought you didn't believe in this stuff?"

"Curious, that's all." Vera pretended to count the dessert forks.

"The needle swung clockwise, in wide circular motions over your photograph. Congratulations — it will be a girl. I even volunteered my hand afterwards. The needle stopped dead, wouldn't budge. No children. I'm sorry."

"Since when do you believe in medieval charms and oracles?"

"When it suits me!"

"Yeah. When are you going to tell them the real reason they'll never see a grandchild from you?"

Tomé frowned and glanced toward the door. He lowered his voice to a whisper.

"It's complicated." He deflected the question with an evasive sweep of his hand and averted his gaze from Vera.

"It's also complicated for everyone else," Vera said, tensing up her eyebrows.

Tomé turned to look into Vera's eyes.

"How complicated is it for you then?" He slowed down his words and delivered them with extra care.

With a handful of cutlery held in mid-air, Vera turned away.

"I know it must have been difficult being kicked out at sixteen after they caught you in bed with your boyfriend. But time does play jokes on us, doesn't it? So ironic that years later he becomes your husband." Tomé paused to chuckle.

Vera remained still and silent.

Tomé cleared his throat and became serious again.

"How come it took you so many years, and getting married, before we heard from you again?"

Vera crouched to stare inside the lower cupboard shelves at the winter preserves with their bright orange, green, and burgundy palette of soothing glows.

No one could imagine how complicated her life had become after she had been kicked out of her home. Tomé had still been playing with Lego and toy trains, too young to confide in. Delfim's parents had him sent away to an undisclosed boarding school. Two weeks later she found herself carrying news she was pregnant. The dark alleys she had travelled to disentangle herself from her despair remained etched in her memory. To this day it still paralyzed her to witness the atrocities people committed against their children. The little and the large abandonments of daily life, from 'Here are five movies, sweetheart, this should keep you occupied' to 'Any minute now Papa should be back from the game. He will play with you then I'm sure.'

Not even her husband understood the depth of her

resistance to bearing a child. She, a teenager on the street, he moving from the best private school to the best university. Years later, he tracked her down on the opposite side of the country and brought her back. To him it was all too simple. "The point of love between two people is to widen the circle and create someone else to love." Easy for him to say. About now he would be halfway across the Atlantic ferrying separated families, restless spirits, sun seekers hopping from continent to continent ahead of the frost snapping at their heels.

Vera sensed her brother staring at her back for an answer and turned.

"She'll die miserable and without her last wish," she remarked with a sigh. "But I just don't think I can do it. It's too much."

"You can't let your happiness depend on someone else's agenda." Tomé walked over and stood behind her. He squeezed her shoulder. "For all the hard knocks you've had, do you wish you'd never been born?"

Vera rose quickly from her crouched position and leaned on the kitchen counter. The question left her without breath and empty of answers.

"I know you'd be a great mother. Delfim knows it. Everyone does. Trust. *You* will be a great mother."

Vera smiled, placed the palm of one hand over her brother's chest and leaned her head on his shoulder. She let him embrace her.

"What's taking you so long? Do you children need help?" Mother walked in, hands on her hips.

o

"Mother, the cake looks marvellous."

"The Chef continues in top form." Tomé blew Mother a kiss.

"Thank you." Mother smiled, pleased. "Leave also room for the *rabanadas* after. Will you cut me a tiny slice of cake, on the orange peel side, Tomé?"

"Sure, Mother, sure. Don't want to slice the broad bean and be responsible for baking next year's *Bolo-Rei?*" Tomé laughed, nervous. The family joined in his laughter.

"Hope not, son. I'll likely not be here next year. If I slice the broad bean you'll be out of luck."

"Come on, Mother, don't be depressing," Tomé said with a cheerful tilt to his voice. "We'll all be here, and who knows, maybe more of us."

"More of us?" Father awoke from his outward-gazing slumber.

Mother widened her eyes. Both parents stared at Tomé with expectation.

He shrugged, offering a conspicuous grin followed by a teasing wink at his sister.

The parents' inquiring gazes shifted to Vera.

A mouth full of cake, unable to utter a word, she denied any responsibility for the news with a vehement, flat out, wave of her hands. For emphasis she swept her head in short denial swings.

Vera turned to her brother and grimaced.

"If one prays enough one must remain hopeful and believe in magic to row against the currents. That's an undercurrent of faith, isn't it?" Tomé mumbled to his parents, his mouth now also half-full of cake. Then he sent an apologetic glance to Vera.

"Of course, of course," Father said with a dismissive turn of his head and a refocus on the outside rain.

Her mother appeared deflated by the false hope of his riddle.

"Looks like I found the *brinde*," said Tomé more loudly than necessary as he picked from his mouth the coin-sized paper mush wrapping the pin.

"How come you always find the good-luck charm?" Vera shook her head in disbelief.

Their attention went to his fingertips, where he unfolded a red automobile pin with a slight dent from his bite.

"Good Lord. Another car for your collection. Sure sign of a prosperous year ahead."

"Don't count on it, Father. Must be second-hand. It's already dented," Tomé laughed, showing them the tooth marks. He pinned it to his sweater.

o

"Definitely malleable." Vera squeezed the package a little and then pretended to sniff it. She bumped the package in the air determining its weight. "Clothes for sure." She smiled in triumph at Mother, waiting for a confirming nod.

"You're spoiling the fun. Surprise is the purpose of a gift. Give up on this guessing game." With unconcealed satisfaction, Mother grinned. This year's game leaned in her favour.

"We can't stop this guessing, it's a tradition. Come on, throw us a hint," demanded Tomé.

"Ah . . . some traditions you don't mind, son?"

Tomé shrugged and offered a sheepish smile.

"Is it spandex yoga leggings, Mother?" Although unlikely, the idea crossed Vera's mind. Next in her mind: sexy underwear. This time she kept the thought to herself. During the first ten years of Vera's married life, her mother must have believed the lack of offspring related to lack of seductive triggers. But Mother had stopped giving her scandalous lingerie for Christmas a few years back.

An exaggerated sigh of defeat and a shrug of the shoulders announced that Vera had given up. She peeled the tape, careful not to tear the folds of the paper. Inside, she found a tiny red polka-dot wetsuit with matching cotton shorts, the lace worn at the hem.

"It was your favourite. You refused to wear anything else at the beach when you were two." Her mother wrung the hands tucked in her lap in quick nervous motions and stared at her with expectant eyes.

"Mother, that's sweet."

Vera almost remembered struggling into the outfit, limbs refusing to be confined by the sleeves, flailing in protest, her mother gently easing her into the suit. She is shaking off her mother's hands and looking out to sea. Mother and Father submersed to their necks, holding hands, the link of their fingers slipping; Mother and Father in troubled waters, looking to the shore, looking for an anchor, seeing only Tomé and Vera. And a child dressed in the red polka-dot wetsuit playing by the shore, her ankles scarcely wet, building sandcastles. Vera's child. The grandparents waving, the grandchild waving back, reinvented flesh of themselves staying on. The child's face soothing her grandparents' fears, fears of the emptying tide swallowing them. The grandparents surviving in the grandchildren's dimples, their stories engraved in memory. Vera sitting down on the sand beside the child to tell her childhood tales, distant reflections of her past, of the grandparents.

"I kept a chest full. A different outfit from every year of your childhood." Mother's voice trembled.

Vera pictured herself easing her child's resistance to squeezing into the wetsuit by telling her about the time Grandmother pulled Mommy from the sea, that Grandmother had saved the polka-dot suit just for her. Vera heard her child ask who this grandmother was. When would she ever meet her? Cradling the garment to her chest, Vera reached for her mother's hand and heard herself say, "It's the perfect gift, Mother. It will look lovely on her."

LOVE & MEDICAL MIRACLES

Néné, underneath the bridge, wakes up to honking cars marooned in the Monday morning traffic. As he pushes aside a blanket of newspapers and cardboard, the inadvertent swing of his elbow jabs Tó. Curled next to him, Tó complains. Néné tugs at his friend's pockets for a hard candy, but instead scores cigarette butts and beer bottle lids. Disappointed, he blows his nose on his mud-caked sleeve. Tó yells at him to shut up. With half-open eyes Néné follows a yacht sailing along the bay. He debates the likelihood of breakfast. Should he steal a tasteless, bruised apple from Laurinda Coração, certain she will turn a blind eye, or should he nab a banana, his favourite fruit, from Zé Mau? Zé Mau will huff and puff after him with a broom, and if he gets caught, Zé Mau will lift him by the ears until he drops the banana. "If you are old enough to steal you are old enough to work." Zé Mau will waste no time pulping the banana with his fat feet to prove his point before sending him off with a boot. "There's no free lunch in this world, little scoundrel."

An intense glare of light tingles the skin on Néné's cheeks. Binoculars glint at him from further up the shoreline. He shrugs, accustomed to the exotic-animal treatment, and stares back. This early in the morning he's too molasses-lazy to jump off his perch, race along the pathway, and demand money: the automatic tax levied on tourists snapping his picture. This morning he coughs and pulls phlegm from the bottom of his chest, aiming the spit at those binoculars. For emphasis he also gives them the bird. The phlegm rises in an arc, lands in the water and disappears.

o

Pale and frail, in the immensity of the hospital bed with a view of *Cristo Redentor*, Jeremy lies lost in the bedsheets. Lively colours radiate from toys that have sat idle on his bedside table, chair, ever since they arrived with him weeks ago. Teddy bears, remote-controlled trucks, race cars, a space city built of Lego blocks he can only stare at when propped up by a float of pillows.

"Doctor, how much longer?"

"We are trying our best."

"Please."

On hearing voices in his room, Jeremy stirs. His mother shushes the father. The father and the surgeon leave. Jeremy struggles to lift one eyelid at a time, a shopkeeper lifting an iron shutter at the start of the day.

His mother settles him up on the pillow, careful not to jostle the arm attached to the IV tube. She opens a book and reads aloud the first line from Aladdin: "Ah I come from a land, from a faraway place, where the caravan camels roam . . ."

Jeremy closes his eyes. The fingers in his hand unfurl in slow motion and the hand crawls above the sheets mimicking a feeble insect in search of the nest of his mother's hand.

o

Néné walks down the street biting into a banana. In a shop window, a remote-controlled ambulance grabs his attention. It isn't the kind of toy he ever lucks into foraging in the dumpsters of rich Copacabana. He stumbles across cars without wheels, the odd piece of Lego . . . nothing as shiny and colourful as the ambulance. He continues on to the construction site where Tó carts buckets of cement up and down stairways. If Néné convinces the foreman to take him on and if he works hard today, he will earn enough to buy the ambulance.

He joins Tó carting buckets of cement. Néné tells him about the ambulance. The bucket bounces against his leg, bruising his skin. His palms burn. The wire handle sinks into his flesh. He uses both hands. His legs tremble, his steps strain to maintain control, and his heart stings, threatening to burst. He trips on a step and spills the bucket. The foreman forces him to work the rest of the morning without pay.

"Yu ain't getting out of here before yu make up for the wasted cement. Do yu think it grows on trees?"

Néné wonders, maybe if he stopped sucking on those

cigarette butts he finds he would have the strength to carry the buckets next time.

At the end of the morning, the foreman slaps a bun with butter into Néné's hands and sends him away with an unconvincing kick on his behind.

"Don't show yur face before yu learn to lift a bucket," he yells and turns his face away from the child to hide a smile.

o

The doctor clears his throat and fidgets with the stethoscope before saying, "I don't want to raise false hopes."

"Look, I hope this isn't about more money. We'll do everything humanly possible to keep Jeremy alive." The father motions to pull his wallet from his breast pocket.

"Please," the doctor protests, lifting his hands in objection. "The odds of finding the ideal match are steep but we have an immaculate delivery record."

"I'm well aware of your success, Doctor. That's the reason we flew here. Any bit of hope is better than nothing." The father furrows his brows for emphasis.

"The best prognosis won't offer Jeremy a normal life. You must understand the limitations. The transplant won't deliver miracles."

"Hope never dies, Doctor." Jeremy's mother lifts her eyes from his sallow face and stares at the doctor. Her fingers coil the rosary around her wrists to a knot.

The doctor remains silent.

"Love will bring him to full life. You see his will to live, don't you, Doctor?" She shows a photograph of Jeremy laughing, ruddy cheeks soaring high on a swing.

o

Néné sits by the water, legs dangling over the seawall, puffing on a dirty cigarette butt. With his eyes, he follows the twirl of current on the surface, playing his game of identifying debris floating on the murky water. The plastic bags and aluminum cans prove easiest, balloons harder. He has spotted bodies. He has heard them scream, falling off the bridge in the middle of the night.

Two men sit further down the wall, unwrap their lunch. Their white coats stand out in this grey, dirty part of town. They wave to him. He waves back. Tó is afraid of them. "They dress like ghosts and smell like cough drops," Tó says when he sees the men, quickly walking the opposite way. Not Néné. He likes them. The men have given him and his friends stickers, chocolates, just so they can prickle their fingers, "to test your health and make sure you grow up to be the mechanic you want to be," they said last week with a friendly tussle of his black curls.

Today, when they call him over, waving a slice of pizza, Néné tosses the unfinished cigarette butt into the current and joins them. They place a can of Guava on his lap, which he opens with a satisfying pop and a fizz. The ripe banana he tucks in his pocket for dinner.

Néné chews the ham and pineapple pizza with gusto and measures up the shiny ambulance with a mesmerized stare.

"Wanna turn on the siren?"

"With the blue and red lights screaming?" His eyes light up.

"Sure thing." They laugh.

He stands up. He can't believe his luck. A soft whistle

disguises his nervous excitement as he approaches the ambulance.

Inside the ambulance one of the men opens the glove compartment to reveal the usual assortment — road maps, flashlight, chewing gum. He pops a piece of gum into his mouth and tosses the child another. Néné scrutinizes the colourful panel of switches. He turns around to inspect the stretcher and the maze of tubes and bottles at the rear. He releases a subtle whistle of awe when from nowhere a hand weighs on his shoulder and another covers his mouth.

o

Balloons hang from the ceiling. A half-dozen eyes stare at the body emerging from the anaesthetic's torpor. His first eyelid opens to spotlights brightening the air in the room. Jeremy's mother covers him in kisses.

"Congratulations, Jeremy!" the surgeon says.

Jeremy ventures a smile.

The surgeon addresses the father: "The intervention went well but we'll have to monitor him."

"How can we thank you, Doctor?" The father clutches the surgeon's hand. "We are eternally indebted." A tear collects in the fold of the father's eye.

"We would like to thank the family who made this miracle possible, Doctor. Their generosity saved a precious life," the mother says as she places a toy train in Jeremy's lap.

"Identities remain confidential. To prevent emotional complications, you see." The doctor twists the stethoscope around his gloved wrists.

Jeremy's mother kisses him on the forehead and drops to

her knees. "Thank you Lord, for blessing our Jeremy with another miraculous chance." She closes her eyes and raises the dangling rosary in religious benediction.

"It will be a great pleasure to make a substantial donation for that latest ultrasound machine," the father says with a friendly smack on the surgeon's back as they leave the room to conclude the conversation.

For the first time in months Jeremy reaches for his burgundy teddy bear and, smiling, informs his kneeling mother, he is hungry. She leans closer and strokes his cheeks, not ruddy, yet looking as though one day, God willing, they might be.

ANOTHER SUNDAY

"Goaaal . . ." the two men screamed, jumping in the air, locked in a joyous embrace. Green and white striped flags waved. Tico fished a whistle from his back pocket.

"We scored, kid. Blow your whistle, too," Tico called to his child, a few steps away near the wire fence, playing with the club mascot, a stuffed lion, and building a pyramid of cigarette butts gathered from the ground. The child obliged, blew on the whistle dangling against his chest, quickly returning to his play.

The Lions, the visiting team, had just scored a header following a corner kick, the ball grazing the inside post and kissing the net.

After the exuberant hopping in each other's arms, the two men in the stands shrank back with awkward grins.

"Pardon me! I'm Tico Esteves." Tico, his smile missing a front tooth, wiped the sweat trickling down his bare chest with the tail of the team's flag.

"Don't mention it. I'm Senhor Couto." Senhor Couto straightened his suit, readjusted his green silk tie. A half-burnt cigarette drooped from the corner of his mouth and braided a thin string of grey into the gull-speckled summer sky.

They returned their attention to the playing field in time to see a striker from their team outrun the Eagles' defence and sprint to the goal before being tackled from behind.

"Murderer!" Tico's fist shook, eager to offer the player a taste of his knuckles.

"They have the manners of butchers. No wonder their jerseys are stained red." Senhor Couto laughed, proud of his wit. In the commotion of the visiting fans jumping and elbowing, the dangling cigarette, unfinished, fell from his mouth and he stamped it out with the heel of his polished shoe. As if he too were one of the midfielders in the game, he side-kicked the stomped cigarette down the steps where it rolled toward the child.

On the turf, the rival teams chased the round leather, tempers inflated. They battled for the pride of their aficionados. The outcome of the ninety-minute contest would decide their fans' taste of glory for the year and would affect the mood of marriages, of cities, of the entire nation.

"Come here, kid! Let me show you an important rule in soccer."

The child raised his head. He stuffed the back pocket of

his black shorts with one last cigarette butt. Then, clutching his stuffed lion, he wobbled up the two steps to his father. Tico raised the child to his shoulders, placing his flag in the child's free hand.

The child stared at the pole in his hand, struggling to lift the flag above his head. He scrutinized the men around him to mimic the sway of their flags. With a strained grunt, he dropped the stuffed lion from the other hand in order to wave the small flag above his head. He grinned, pleased with the smile of approval radiating from his father.

"That-a-boy! Today's lesson: the offside. When their monkey-head striker stands behind our defence, be sure to raise the flag and yell, offsiiide! This referee hand-picked a cross-eyed donkey for a linesman. We can't take chances."

From the vantage point of his father's shoulders, the child gazed in wonder at the palette of white and green colours in the stands next to him, the effusive mood that bobbed the sea of heads at his eye level, the yelling and singing that washed in constant waves over the stadium. Then, slowly, his attention drifted to a flock of gulls riding the thermal above and he watched their effortless frolic in the blue sky.

Senhor Couto smiled.

"My friend, don't you think that's a bit complicated for a boy his age?"

"Not at all. His mother already drags him to church, teaching him about saints, angels, and the Saviour. This is peanuts in comparison."

A goal down, and incited by the fans' deafening shriek, the hometown Eagles increased the pace, applied pressure, seized control of the midfield. Their hero, a striker nicknamed Black Panther, in a supreme dribble that drew an "oh . . . oh . . ."

of reverence from the crowd, freed himself from the vigilance of the green-jerseyed defenceman. He gained speed and raced toward the goal. Two paces inside the penalty box, Black Panther swung his leg to strike a sure shot. Another defenceman, in a last desperate effort, hooked Black Panther's foot from behind and the striker collapsed onto the turf. The impact echoed across the stadium and sparked an outraged shriek from the red-coloured jerseys. The referee ran to the penalty mark.

"Foul, foul! Can you believe your God-given eyes? Black Panther can't stand a nudge. A porcelain doll playing a man's game. Chew a few steaks before standing on your crystal feet." Tico jabbed an accusing finger at Black Panther. "Should have waved offside, kid. Grave mistake." Tico lifted the child off his shoulders and onto the cement steps. Startled, the child bit his lower lip and frowned. He settled down to search for the stuffed lion he had dropped earlier among the forest of legs now towering around him. At the same time, and as if struck by lightning, Tico fell on his knees next to his son, arms raised to the sky, imploring divine justice. The son, worried, hurried a step down nearer the wire fence, clinging to his toy.

Senhor Couto stomped his feet. The veins in his neck bulged. He fired his words at Black Panther.

"This isn't ballet. Don't expect to land on fuzzy arms after your fancy tiptoeing." Senhor Couto twisted the tip of his moustache and hissed his anger.

Tico returned to his feet.

"Blind crow! You need a white cane!" Tico yelled, and frenetic, he wagged his finger an inch from his own nose, informing the referee of his impairment.

"I bet those butchers will fill your fridge with shepherd cheese and sausage." Senhor Couto flexed his arm and clenched his fist at the referee.

Black Panther appeared more irritated at his soiled white shorts, which he brushed off with fierce strokes, than the unfair play. After a delay that included kissing the ball, patting the adjacent grass, and staring at the goalkeeper, he placed the globe of leather on the chalk mark and stepped back several paces to gain momentum for the kick. The goalkeeper swayed his outstretched arms between the goal posts, his fluttering wings ready to swoop in the right direction and capture the ball. Tico gripped Senhor Couto's arm and sank desperate fingers into his flesh.

"Easy, man. You're tearing the sleeve off my jacket. Nothing will come of the penalty. You're religious, I expect?"

"I can't bear this torture." Tico blessed himself and turned his back to the field, his body trembling like a wet sparrow. "God forgive me, but I promise to kiss our goalkeeper if he stops this shot." Tico fell to his knees again.

Senhor Couto nearly twisted the ends right off his moustache and tilted on his toes to find a clear opening among the expectant heads in front.

"This is no time to cheer! Stop blowing the whistle, kid, and come here. Let's put your mother's catechism to good use." Tico forced the child to drop the stuffed lion again and kneel beside him. Together, hands pressed in prayer, they chanted.

"Our Father who art in Heaven . . ."

A cathedral-like silence reigned over the stadium until the home crowd's abrupt and festive roar shook the stands.

"I've told you, kid, it's a waste of time to spend your life in church. God doesn't listen anyway." Tico nudged his son back towards the fence. Stuffed lion clasped to his chest, he crouched in his own small universe of cigarette butts, happy to leave the loud intensity of adult games.

"Come on boys, let's get back in this game. We suffered a cheap goal, that's all. Let's show them the ABCs of soccer," Senhor Couto shouted in encouragement to the green-jerseyed players. "Care for a smoke? Finest medicine for the nerves on the planet." He offered a cigarette from his shiny metal case and Tico snatched a smoke with a swift and satisfying snap of his fingers.

"See this?" Tico pointed to his missing tooth. "Last year's Cup, some ass dared to call one of our Lions out there a kitten."

"A kitten? That's some nerve!" Senhor Couto shook his head, tossing the still-burning match at his feet.

"We lost the game but I never felt better in my life. I showed the guy that the Lion reigns on and off the field." Tico curled his hand into a fist, cracking his knuckles with a domino effect.

"They need to learn some respect," Senhor Couto emphasized with the sway of his head.

"Yeah, I lost a tooth but the ass lost his whole front keyboard. He sure crawled away like a wet cat holding his tail between his legs. I proved who was right, hey?"

"Sure did!" Senhor Couto mumbled with an uncomfortable grin and a quick turn of his body toward the play in the field.

"You'll never hear that guy chirp again that the lion's roar resembles a stray cat's meow on a shanty roof!" Tico rolled his sleeves a notch further up his arm and punched the sky above him to emphasize his point before he too turned his attention to the game.

o

The mid-afternoon sun beat down on the stands and the occasional cry of a low-flying gull sounded above the crowd. During a momentary pause in the game to assist a hurt player, Tico folded a newspaper and improvised a hat for his child.

"Players can't imagine the sacrifices a man faces to place bread on a family's plate and yet afford to be here, providing a little encouragement to our team," Senhor Couto said, wiping his forehead with the back of his hand.

Tico nodded with a solemn face. "God forgive me the times I robbed a little on the coin I bring home from the quarry shift to make sure I don't miss a game. My missus would strangle my sparrow neck if she ever suspected I shortchange her and the kid on the grocery money."

Senhor Couto looked Tico in the eye and placed his hand on his shoulder.

"A sign of a dedicated Lion, Tico. There are less and less of your stock. The dedication, the sacrifices required to be here cheering our boys. Yes, those are true evidence of character. The young fans today don't understand true love for a team."

"Absolutely. But my boy here —" Tico pointed to the child by the wire fence, demolishing the pyramid of cigarette butts with a punch of his fist and starting to build it up again "— he's being brought up right. Hasn't missed a match from the time he was old enough to sit on his behind without falling over."

Senhor Couto, measuring the boy in his oversized green and white jersey, blew a curtain of smoke toward the child and asked, "What's the best team in the world, kid?"

The child, immersed in his cigarette butt play, did not respond.

"Hey kid, the gentleman asked you a life-and-death question!" Tico poked him with the pole of his flag before he turned to Senhor Couto and added, "He's on the right track. His mother can't shove tomatoes down his throat. Loves lettuce and cucumbers instead. Isn't that something?" Tico nudged Senhor Couto with his elbow, breaking into a muffled laugh. "She spends her life in doctors' offices trying to fix the poor kid. They tell her it sounds like acute Lionism and there is no vaccine they've heard of."

Senhor Couto gave his thumbs up to the kid and chuckled in amusement.

"I say, nothing like slipping candy into his pocket every time he refuses to eat anything red. Must set the priorities straight, isn't that right, kid?" Tico winked at the child and tossed him a peppermint candy.

o

Five minutes from the final blow of the referee's whistle, the score continued tied at one. The green jerseys pressured. Only a victory would bring the Cup home. Except for the goalkeeper, twenty-one players crowded the Eagles' side of the field. Little time remained and the players surrendered their hearts to despair, ignoring the dressing room tactics. The ball, ballooned with precipitous frequency into the penalty box, triggered the players' stampede for its possession. The coaches, disgruntled, screamed instructions while hopping up and down the sideline.

After one desperate drop kick into the penalty box a Lions' striker sprinted side by side with an Eagles' defenceman. In the shoulder-to-shoulder battle for control of the leather, the green striker tumbled to the ground. He rolled on the grass in a writhing whirl, clutching the side of his ribs and howling as though a bull had rammed him. The green-jerseyed players swarmed the referee, demanding the highest punishment. The referee waved his hands, clearing the play while running in the opposite direction.

"Foul! Do you need glasses, you son of a punctured rotten ball?" Senhor Couto yelled, his middle finger aimed at the referee.

The infuriated green-jersey fans moved closer to the barbed-wire fence and shook it with ruthless zest. Tico rushed to lift the child into his arms and away from the exalted tempers, the pounding feet.

"See that ass in black, my son? Never trust a man in black — priests aside, of course. He just robbed our team of a penalty." The child looked with dedicated eyes to his father and nodded in agreement.

The aficionados showered the soccer field with broken bottles and stones. Some attempted to climb over the barbed-wire fence, unaware of ripping clothes and bleeding flesh. Even Senhor Couto joined in, grabbing the wire fence and shaking it without mercy.

"Mother, wherever you rest in heaven, I hope you are napping. A man must do what a man must do!"

The child, perched on Tico's arms, one arm clenching the stuffed lion, fished old tickets and wrinkled cigarette butts from his pockets. He squashed them in his fist, swung his arm as far back as he could, nearly losing his balance, and pitched his paper crumble in the referee's direction. Fury blazed his eyes.

"That-a-boy!" exclaimed Tico. "You'll sure never let me down. I see a strong rib of mine in you."

"Give him a few more years and he will be throwing the real

stuff at the referee's nozzle," Senhor Couto said with a curt approving nod, stomping on another half-finished cigarette.

The referee whistled the interruption of the play while a ball-boy crew cleared the bottles and stones from the field. A few gulls seized the opportunity to swoop down to the sidelines and inspect the content of rolling paper bags and food wrappers. This far into the game, players' muscles had been failing to respond with the necessary swiftness and both teams, glad for the interruption, ambled to the sidelines to douse their faces with water bottles, thankful for the opportunity to catch their breath.

Signaling two minutes of play remaining, the referee glanced at his watch and whistled the restart of the game. The Lions' fans, revealing the face of disquiet, anticipated the imminent sentence. Their chins drooped. Their faith was silenced. Everything appeared lost until, in a last impulsive effort, a frustrated Lion midfielder fired a cannon shot. The inspired kick carried the seal of a goal. It described a curve over the wall of bodies crowding the penalty area and hit the post. The stadium fell silent as the ball bounced in a lateral trajectory and rushed along the goal line, undecided on which side to drop.

The helpless goalkeeper, arms paralyzed in surrender, feet glued to the turf, glanced over his shoulder and watched.

Tico, using Senhor Couto's shoulders for leverage, jumped in the air blowing his lungs empty. The ball, unaffected, followed the chalk line and bounced off the opposite post into the goalkeeper's arms, who welcomed the leather like a father welcoming a returning child. He kissed the ball and raised his eyes to heaven.

The final whistle blew.

o

Eyes downcast, feet kicking discarded garbage, Tico and Senhor Couto walked away from the stadium puffing on cigarettes, jostled by the crowd of disheartened fans. Tears ran down their cheeks.

"This season alone these one-legged dodos already gave me two ulcers to add to my collection of pains. We pay their weight in gold expecting them to give us some of life's joys and they prance off the field like it hasn't deflated our entire week," Senhor Couto said, shrugging, unbothered by a splash of guano that had just landed on his shoulder.

Despite the smoke blown into his face and making him cough, the child, in Tico's arms, attempted to wipe his father's tears with his newspaper hat. In his apprehensive haste, he dropped his stuffed Lion. Preening his head over his father's shoulder, the child watched the army of feet trample his mascot until it disappeared from view. He glanced at the two men immersed in their laments and, with a sigh, returned to his task of drying his father's tears with the newspaper hat.

"Good God, these Lions are my ruin. Nail my heart to the cross, leave me to bleed, rather than live through this agony every Sunday. It takes a team like these Lion kittens to make a man like me cry. Didn't shed a single tear at my father's funeral to set a good example to my kid and look at me now bawling like a baby." Tico turned his face away from the child who seemed shocked to a frowning silence by the gravity of the moment.

"Don't think of it. A man isn't made of stone." Senhor Couto sniffled and cleared his nose with a swipe of his arm, leaving a glistening streak on the sleeve of his black suit.

The men discussed the missed shots, the bad luck that, with religious persistence, had persecuted their team for decades. They concluded a curse had been placed on the Lions. In the theatre of their minds they replayed the game's tragic moments, as if for an instant they believed they might change the past.

"But I'm not taking this bullshit anymore." Tico looked his son in the eye, squinting to find him through the grey curtain of smoke wrapping his gaze. "You'll be a soccer player when you grow up and you'll kick that ball exactly as I teach you. We'll never lose a game then." Tico smiled, inflated with hope, lodging a slobbering kiss on his son's cheek. The child swiveled his head away from his father's embrace, away from the crush of people carrying them out of the stadium grounds. He fixed his eyes on the summer blue sky and his gaze glazed over. The men once again became lost in the recounting of the afternoon's tragedies on the turf.

The son, absorbed in his own dreams, gazed far into the distance where another Sunday disappeared behind the hill and a gull flapped its wings in a steady wave that moved the bird high above the visible horizon.

NOT WRITTEN IN PENCIL

Arial and I weren't bad people or nothing, just different spark plugs misfiring under the same hood. It's like this. Arial lived for now. I lived for tomorrow's bills.

I'm not thinking she exemplified a young case of Alzheimer's or nothing. You might think she slipped to forgetful on her wedding vows, but I say no. No more forgetful than most, if the scandal rags are anything to go by. She lived for the tick of every second. So much that she would forget details like coming back home at night. Now that I give it a proper think, Arial was a genuine Buddhist wearing all prayer bells and whistles and surely counting on the champaka incense smokescreen around her. Two times out of three I would find her cross-legged like she was just there contemplating every-thing and bothered by nothing. Including filling up the fridge and feeding the kiddo.

o

And me? Like I told Arial the day I married her and the day she gave birth to our kiddo: I don't write my commitments in pencil. I'm a guy who doesn't forget things from yester-day, even less from last year, including my free Christmas tune-up offer for the loyal customer at the auto shop that I'd like to forget but had put my word to. I'll slave through the night if need be until the job is done and the customer is smiling.

I've got memory all right, memory so deep in my DNA that I even remember things from the crib. My mother hosing me good with water to cool down my toddler tantrums or biting my wrists to make sundial marks with her teeth. Somewhere in her bones she carried the genes of a prankster. Locking me out on the balcony after dark as she laughed with her nose pressed to the window and dry-mouthing for off-season spooky effect that she could smell the bogeyman coming closer and closer to snatch me. All for not thinking to take my rubber boots to school in the storm and muddying up my new sneakers. Don't worry, I didn't shed a tear and give her the pleasure. Anyways, the monster that's gonna scare me at Halloween hasn't been born yet. I like to know things far down the road, and walk with my high beams on.

o

It might have worked all right between Arial and me. I mean, maybe I could have been converted to living with other men in the picture if we had a merry-go-round agreement, if she'd kept it quiet and covered her tracks. After all, according to *People* magazine, everyone is sleeping with everyone else and it's been like that since the cave. Or, like Greg at the auto shop says, the snake and apple. I don't read the Bible, I'm allergic to apostles of any brand, but that's what Greg told me and I believe that guy. He's been more strictly married than everyone I know added together and he doesn't show one white hair for it. He keeps spare parts on the side, of course. "A regular oil change to keep the engine purring smooth," he says with a wink.

I could even have lived with that "being in the now" creed if she didn't forget that I could get pretty slivery about other men. I ain't all crocodile skin. Even though I go to the gym every day after work, under all this brawn I carry a few raw nerves. If folk reckon I'm stupid or a buffoon just 'cause I don't use polished Rolls-Royce words and could care less for the rules of the grammatical road, hell think again. Anyways, I read between the lines, and that's where I get the best mileage.

I also don't want you to get the wrong impression or nothing. I'm no saint myself. I'm tempted by flesh waggling from the right places. I whistle once in a while. With class, mind you. Never when I sensed Arial around. I still know what respect means. But my eyes aren't on a leash, they like to follow the jiggling. It's like they got a mind of their own. Can't help it. They say it's our reptile brain. A survival thing. I mean it's like opening up the newspaper and admiring the Sunshine Girl, instinctual. Maybe I've been hanging around those voluptual garage calendars for too long. But I'm more whistle than action. I don't try to track the babes down in ads like, "Gorgeous, I caught ya smiling my way at checkout number 9. Wanna go for cappucciiiinoo?"

○

Problem is Arial had such a soft heart she couldn't say no to nothing. She was probably sleeping with those guys 'cause they were lonely and she just had to cheer them up. Problem number two is, because Arial wasn't so expert at keeping her escapades under tight wraps, I would end up sitting down to drink with my plumber buddy Cody only to find out later that the laughter in the place was directed at me. Problem number three, once in a blue moon she would forget I was going to pick up our son from school and I would get to the house and, you know, drop the kid and my jaw at the sight in the bedroom. Well, it isn't a big deal when the kid is two, three, but at eleven, twelve, it's a blister to explain.

Arial, hiccupping and wearing a fresh change of tears, "If you had a heart you'd find compassion for me," she said, packing up for another retreat where for the right coin they would supply compassion for her straying self because "No one is perfect, Ernie." She also assured me she must love herself first before she could love me right. Left me her mint-condition pocket book of Buddha wisdoms on the bedside table with a note advising me to chant my anger away and overcome my pride. Two more strings of prayer flags decorated the balcony railings when I came out with the kiddo for our regular butter and toast breakfast with a view of the freeway. "Mom gone to Buddha camp, again?" the kiddo would ask, biting his lip, burying his mind into another book and strangely uninterested in admiring the monster dirt trucks stuck in the town crawl. "Yep," I would say and give him an extra dollop of strawberry jam when he was four, not so much now he's thirteen.

o

I remember when Arial waltzed into the garage that first time with a smile that certified she could not ever hurt a fly even if she tried. The sight of her red freckles peeking under the car wheels made me bang my head on the transmission bolt right there and then. Nice spill. After I cleaned myself up she hugged me, saying, don't keep hurting yourself, dear, we need you to keep the universe well-oiled and turning, and I knew there was a woman with high standards out there besides my mother, who always said it was a blessing I was good with my hands.

The first year of marriage, Arial brought me flowers and sushi rolls to the shop, leaving every guy drooling over her paper-thin mustard gypsy skirt. "You hit the jackpot this time, Ernie." Greg poked me with a freshly-licked finger to my bare shoulder, making sizzling, overheated radiator sounds every time he touched my new Buddha tattoo.

Arial would sit on the hydraulic jack meditating, changing the vibration of the place in a heartbeat, and I swear, making even the nuts twirl smoother on their thread. The way Arial smiled made the shop crew put the brakes on cursing and feel all Ghandi about it. She even modelled a disarming way of getting delinquent accounts to pay up on the phone by explaining to them the arithmetics of karma and the higher interest of such an equation. "Not worth the hell realms haunting you for eternity, hon," she would tell them while blowing me a kiss. That was the most peaceful way I've ever seen someone get another to cough up a debt.

I too am a peaceful guy. I stay out of trouble. You wouldn't catch me marching around with flowers around my neck, waving the chicken legs sign in the air. You don't bother me, I don't bother you. Course, a finger, once in a while, for those asses on the road doesn't hurt nobody. Still, I surprised myself when last year I started losing my temper at the bar, like once when I heard someone whisper my name and next day, they had to go looking for their front tooth in the lost and found box.

But then last month I started to get edgy with the kiddo.

o

Even the kiddo couldn't be the crazy glue to save the wedding ring from sliding off her delicate hand. God bless the boy though, he tried hard this last year by shutting his mouth and his door, living out of our way in his gloomy room. I'm not sure if it was the gene factor or the sight of a sore eye but the good coaching I had learned from my mother wasn't working as good on Dale who, unlike his mother, seemed bothered by everything. Looking so high over both of us to the divine or else with eyes wide shut to see her mind more clearly, Arial would take days before she would zoom on Dale's face. By then she pretty much had left kiddo's matters up to me.

I meant well. Can't think of a better way to educate a kiddo to stand up to the inevitable punches of life than by dealing out a few. Life is suffering, all right. Lesson number one. You gotta always pick yourself up, stand with the chin high and carry on. His mother should have liked my curriculum, and I was nearly converted to this Buddhist Warrior path myself. I even tried my mother's balcony trick after he refused to go to school for a week, afraid of some stupid kid bent on punching his face. "Punch back twice as friggin' hard, kiddo," I said, locking the balcony door and leaving him to cool down in the rainstorm. But both the trick and the advice were stale on Dale who's afraid of everything by now and tiptoes around like he has the bogeyman living inside his own home. Still, when I let him off the balcony and told him how lucky he was 'cause he never had a father he never met 'cause he holidayed for life in a jail for attempted murder, he cried in my face and said, "That's horribly sad, Dad." That's when I got suspicious. A wimpy kid afraid of everything? I finally figured out the whole eureka, the boy and me aren't made of the same genes at all, for fuck's sake.

o

Maybe you think Arial was bad business or, like her ex before me said, promiscuous. But you'd be wrong. She carried the plain softest heart. She wouldn't walk by a street person without sparing a handful of coins, emptying her purse and my chances for a Friday T-bone steak dinner. Once, back in that cloudless April when we dated before getting married, I stood outside the change room of a store, colours screaming so bright I kept my sunglasses on. She tried on those Guatemalan dresses with more dyes than two overlapping rainbows in the thralls of rain, when her eyes happened upon this photograph on the wall of a kid sitting at a loom. Mad as a fundamentalist she bolted into the street swearing she would never set foot in that store again. Now, it takes moral fibre to stand up for kids like that.

The night Dale was born, I thought I had a toughie successor carrying on with my genes when he arrived a little ahead of schedule, showing off his mighty mane of manhood, chubby cheeks and all, as if time was no mountain for him. In his first day at home, after his supersonic recovery and hospital stay, I tossed him in the air like a football. "You're a toughie, after your dad. Nothing will get to ya, Son." Arial smiled at me. "Just like Daddy, Dale." Looking in the rear-view mirror, I see a lot more to that smile now.

So many times I had heard the word *promiscuities* tossed around the bar like darts, I asked my buddy to spell it right for me, and I went finger-licking through the dictionary to find out what hid behind the mystery. I mean it could have been a disease or one of those nasty foreign flus, ha, ha. Hell no, it just said something about being mixed up some. I can understand that. Everyone gets mixed up some. And between us, I think it might have been a family thing, the ghost gene. Arial remembers her father away for weeks, jet-setting across the planet from meeting to meeting, while her mother untwisted the knots of her loneliness at the yoga studio and the hairdresser. It might have been the diet, too. They didn't eat that good. Mostly salads, exotic fruits, and unpronounceable fluffy pastries full of atmosphere and zippo meat. Eating that kind of nothingness, no wonder she turned out airy-fairy like her mom, easily blown in every direction. You are what you don't eat. I believe that. Look at me, since I've started the protein supplements, it's like I can't stop growing the brawn. I've got the elephant punch in my repertoire now.

o

I mean, she's been going to a therapist also on my tab for so long she knows everything about feelings, like a car lubricated nice, all instruments and everything working dandy, but that keeps crashing. No rattling bolts in her head. Smooth talk. Says all the right things: "My dark shadow is getting in the way of my higher self, I can't control my pain-body when setting boundaries for my kid . . ." So, I know they'll find nothing wrong with her fuse box. All in all pretty faithful to this marriage, she kept seeing that therapist guy just to flesh things out. Dandy with me. I bought season tickets to the Stampeders and while she lay on the couch for that therapist I sat front row near the cheerleaders with my bud Cody. Despite being old enough to be my father and wearing a respectable mane of grey wisdom, he shouted out along with me some swanky curses at those hard heads that have been throwing the leather around for years and still can't get a pass straight against the Eskimos. The boys' mind jam must be psychological or something. I suggested to Arial she beg her therapist to dispense me a couple of foolproof shouts to apply from the sideline to motor the team along at the western final. They say it's all in the mind. Might make a difference for the boys and the whole city would be happier.

Meanwhile, last month, biting my nails in the stands, I was still hoping for a comeback from the Stamps despite two consecutive fumbles in the end zone by the slow-assed receiver. Things improved in the second quarter after Cody and me jumped up to celebrate a rare twenty-yard run and high-fived each other, though even before my buddy had landed on his feet, he was already busy chatting up the brunette next to him. That's when my eyes zeroed in on the open wallet on the ground between our seats that had spilled a photo of Arial and our kiddo. I pocketed the photo with a turbo glance at the back. "If you love it set it free." Written flowerlike inside a lipstick-drawn red heart.

Well, luckily for Cody I did not have to wait for him to slip on the banana peel of his own memory to break his jaw. I helped him myself in the last quarter when my darling Stamp boys came through with a rare punted ball through the posts and as Cody and me jumped hollering and screaming, I accidentally graced him with a mighty hook to his chin that will leave him without a tongue to brag about his Casanova forays to all his chumps in the bar.

o

So I don't understand why Arial pulled her disappearing Houdini act on us last week and evaporated without a trace. It must take a very confused woman not to appreciate a man so handy with his fists. She had already shown a queasy temperament seeing me stumbling back home again and again late at night with bruises and blood on my face. This little incident with Cody tipped her over the punchline. Not that she was scared of me, exactly. I'd never touch a woman. A guy like that isn't a man.

o

I must say Arial did try to issue marriage and motherhood a good thirteen-year exploration permit. Every year on New Year's Eve she opened up her rosy book of affirmations and read. After, she would turn to me and say, "Ernie, it's a new year and I'm changing my bad karma, I'm going to be a better wife and mother, and I'm going to stop smoking too." And she would go cold turkey for a few weeks in January until one evening, bang, the ashtray overflowed and her exhaust snaked up to the ceiling, making up for the lost time. She shouldn't have tried to change two things at once.

I do some quick marriage math on the fly. Twelve years of Arial seeing a shrink, several lifetime reincarnations with coach Buddha sitting on her shoulder whispering instructions and *enlighting* the way, and still, Arial is Arial. Hmmmm. Anyways, I believe that in her head she too believed she had converted to the monogamous. I say that 'cause she swore she didn't go to bed with more than one fellow at a time.

o

To be fair, on ninety per cent of the marriage equation, which is most of the cake, Arial committed her commitments to me. Unlike my father, at least she has stuck around this far into the toughest game in town. Kind of a drag she occasionally believed in taking weekends and holidays from those commitments in order to renew her strength. Apart from those depressed times when she wavered a little and told me, "Life is written in pencil, Ernie. Thank the Universe for that because that means we can always change our ways." At those times she prescribed herself weeks of wilderness retreating to renew her squeaky spirit in the fresh air and sunshine. And believe me, enlightenment is a damn fancy-shmancy destination, no wonder so very few can land there. Just look at the pile of overdraft warnings from my credit-card jackals.

o

She was bang on about one thing. Things change. Everything is really written in pencil. I can see that now. Like being a father you know, first day of goo-gooing and cooing you think everything is lined up to be heaven and all of a sudden you scare yourself years later when you begin to feel indifferent about your kiddo and then you really scare yourself the day you friggin' hate your kiddo's guts after he tells you, "I wish you weren't my dad." You hear your mother's words spewing from your very mouth, "God-dammit, I curse the day you were born," and you want him out the damn door. He pleads, he's sorry, grabbing on to the friggin' doorknob with all his desperation, but it's too late now, things are going downhill without brakes, and you hit him, and then hit him again and again, you can't stop hitting him even though you recognize the screams from your childhood and you don't know where that rage came from so lickety-split.

Course things change. I can understand all that.

Hell, no. One thing them Buddhists can't change is being dead. That you ain't gonna change much at all. Once someone is dead you are dead forever. And that is written in stone.

AN ABUNDANCE OF FLOWERS

I listen for steps in the corridor, I listen for signs of familiarity. Clap-like steps and I expect my ex-wife in her Birkenstocks. Steps landing like a leaf and I expect my son, poking his anxious head through the door, hoping I'm asleep so he can leave a note saying he dropped by.

Squeaky steps.

It's nurse Kal. He walks in carrying a bundle of daisies to join the rainbow of flowers brightening the room.

"You have more friends than anyone I know, Mr. Burr," nurse Kal says, delivering his professional smile.

I want to remind Kal that flowers are not friends, but remain silent. It's not easy to speak after being hit by lightning.

The white coats call it a stroke. A stroke! There's nothing tender about the occasion. It numbed my right side. Terrible to watch pieces of my body die in instalments.

"How am I supposed to find room for all of these?" Kal sweeps his arm in front of him. A grand gesture. He dreams of becoming an actor, and perhaps of receiving as many bouquets on stage.

The daisies arrive on the first of every month with mechanical punctuality. The card always saying, "Thinking of you . . ." computer-signed in Matisse font, "Your Team at the Agency."

"Give them all away," I slur.

Kal nods, leaves, and walks door to door placing a different bouquet in each room.

I hear exclamations of excitement, fainter and fainter as he moves down the corridor.

o

Five o'clock and feminine footsteps arrive next door. The high heels mark the tic-tac of seconds along the corridor and distract me from the countdown chronometer of the body. She arrives after work to relieve her husband's day shift and to spend the night with her mother. I hear a paper bag crumple. The comforting aromas of cinnamon buns and coffee make their path to my room.

The husband will return after dinner with their two children. They'll play Old Maid together. That's the only time I hear the grandmother laugh. Some nights I can't bear their happiness seeping through the walls. I turn the TV up louder, find a rerun of *Cheers* and try to laugh, too.

More than the drip tube in my vein dispensing spurts of

peace, I need spark and noise in my room to trick the mind into believing I'm not alone. When the staff won't allow TV after hours, I turn to my Walkman, sticking one headphone in my good ear. That's how I fall asleep. I like the voice on my book tape. I imagine tulip-shaped lips whispering in my ear, a tender lock of hair perfuming my face. An angel. My private, undemanding angel. Thank God for technology. Nowadays, we don't need to invoke our imagination to keep us company. All imagining is supplied for a price, and more often than not, found in the mall's bargain bin.

o

A fellow wearing loose clothes, the ones you find on sixties hippies, moved last week into the room on my right. I never hear sounds from there. Never a voice or a bed creaking. It unsettles me. Kal says it's because there's so much noise in my room. Last night I smelled burning incense.

This morning I do not miss the chance to complain. I ask Kal if everything happening next door is still legal.

He nods yes, and smiles.

"Kal," I wriggle the side of my nose that can still wriggle, "that smoke is frankly incensing me." Kal wipes the drool off my chin after kindly waiting for the finish to my slow motion joke.

"Mr. Burr, Mr. Burr . . . it freshens up the air."

"With smoke?"

He shakes his head.

"Want to turn me into pemmican or moccasins?"

Kal reaches for the remote by my bedside and mutes the blaring TV.

"It's heaven next door, Mr. Burr. I can hear my heartbeat any time I walk in there!"

Forget-me-nots from my accountant entered the room in Kal's hand and he is still looking for an impossible space among the flora on the table. He winks, "Still have a way with the ladies, haven't you?"

"Courier them to my grave, will you Kal?"

Kal grimaces and leaves with the head shaking.

The fellow in loose clothes from next door comes into my room and sits cross-legged on a chair, meditating even before I introduce myself. He doesn't say anything, wrapped in a smile. I nod back. For him, I turn off the TV and the radio. For me, I turn on the Walkman. He doesn't even own a strand of hair. Typical for these spiritual types. I can't tell what he is dying of. Faster or slower, we're all dying of one thing or another here. He appears calm, jaw loose. A glimmer waxes his large eyes. Strange. I envy him. He's used to silence. Kal is right. The air and the light in the room appear brighter and taste fresher after he sits in the room for an hour. I suspect he is practising his next life. I already envision him reincarnated and of service as a quiet, high-end air filter.

I know the arrival of a full moon by the howl at the end of the corridor. It's a fellow with a silvery beard and tiny round glasses. At times, he leaves me a whole wheat blueberry muffin with the side serving of a handwritten thought of the day: *If you continually give, you will continually have.* I ask Kal to deliver doughnuts to his room and, even though Kal says he doesn't eat them, this man comes by and says thank you by dropping a note in perfect Chinese calligraphy. That's manners for you. I'll send him two from now on.

I wonder if, after we vacate the planet, he and I will end up in the same afterlife condominium. I wonder if all of us on this floor are destined to end up together. Will we remember each other? Is that the reason why the big mamma with the devil tattoos screams in her sleep, scaring off any angel willing to take her on the final ride in the wind?

The night nurse sits by her bedside lullabying her nightmares to sleep.

o

The day begins. Morning sun highlights my life's accomplishments; golden seals glow at the bottom of certificates and diplomas that cover the walls. Printed red ribbons shine with the touch of first light. The Order of Canada, for political services rendered to the nation, occupies its honourable place in the centre, a tad removed from others for best decorative effect, compliments of Kal. "To remind you of your great achievement, Mr. Burr."

I could sit up by myself with a concert of grimaces and grunts if I tried. Instead, I ring for Kal. I grasp his hand, feeling his warm, sweaty palm lift me up. I cling to it, a little longer than I should, and ask for the newspaper, pretending I have forgotten my hand in his. It wasn't too long ago when I would have punched a man who dared to get that close. As it is, the touch of any skin reminds me I am alive.

I tell him I've been thinking of asking him to stay the night shift too. He could sleep on the fold-out divan. He would save money faster by double-shifting on the side. Who wouldn't like to earn a living by sleeping?

"You ring the bell and the night staff will be here in a wink, Mr. Burr!"

He winks.

o

I pay to have treats brought up from the kiosk downstairs. Pizza, doughnuts, and muffins for staff and my partners in purgatory, slurpies for my rusty jaw. This morning, despite the daily health admonishments from Kal, I'm buying everyone on my floor a doughnut for breakfast. I like Tara, the delivery gal. She walks in little jumps and fills the room with freckles.

Today, I don't recognize her steps. My heart skips a beat. Another little death in my chest. They never warn me when the coffee shop staff move on. Money is the problem. The pay's not enough. I've phoned their manager and offered to double the wages for my favourite employees. But their wage policy is one of the few things my money can't influence. And the managers laugh, "Always joking, Mr. Burr."

By the grin on his face, the young chap who replaced Tara seems to be doing all right and isn't suffering as much as one might imagine from whatever affliction turned his stand-up hair bright blue. Sprinkles of hair dare their first show-off on his chin too. Kurt, according to the name tag, doesn't know where to place the doughnut boxes among the sea of flowers and stands shuffling his feet until he realizes help will not be forthcoming. Tara would have known what to do. I will play marble statue in city square until this kid shows me his true colours. He piles the boxes on my lap, saying, "You must have some appetite!" He offers a nervous laugh and turns brusquely, bumps into the night table. The picture frame, with its photograph of my daughter against exotic jungle trees, crashes to the floor. Kurt loses the pimplish red in his face and turns canvas white. I see my daughter's face through cracks in the glass. Kurt runs out of the room.

My daughter lives in Papua New Guinea delivering medicine to tribes in the hills. The poor die such useless deaths, avoidable with fifty cents of medicine. She can't bear it. She calls me whenever she scrounges up time to access a phone. "You know Daddy, let's make this call meaningful. Ten lives could be saved for the time we chat." Everything I had planned to say dries up in my throat.

o

I can't really complain about this purgatory. Memories around my villa had gelled to dreadful silence. At least here I meet new noises, and there's the flux of other people's visitors. It's like sitting in a café with the comforting sound and sight of other lives orbiting around oneself to keep loneliness at bay.

Without the T V on late at night, I hear the shuffling of the woman patient whose full-time job is to lead the procession of midnight shadows back and forth down the corridor. Is that what nurses mean by telling us to keep up the good work of scaring death away from these premises? In my younger years I did plenty of that useless back and forth, staying busy between what I wanted to do and what I should be doing. It brought on trouble later on. Messed up my heart. Another woman, skin hanging from her arms like a shawl, paces up and down the corridor with a rosary woven through her fingers. She emits a sound that reminds me of bees in a hive. Soothing, on a pain-free day. On the other days, the sound resembles the grinding on tracks of a toy train moved around useless loops by the remote-controlled hand of an insomniac God.

o

I used to laugh at my old aunt Silvia when she confessed to praying for people to ring the doorbell. Cookies, subscriptions, she bought anything they were selling just to keep them talking. She joined the Mormon Church and Jehovah's Witnesses; she opened the door to window cleaners, vacuum salesman, and invited them in for tea.

Tonight, I scroll through the unanswered stored numbers on my cell phone and dial telemarketing companies, their salespeople. It messes them up. I ask how come they never call me anymore. I tell them I find out about their once-in-a-lifetime deals only through my friends. Don't they know there are people out there dying to buy? I purchase baseball and opera tickets, hand-painted floral thimbles and mouth- and foot-painted calendars; I let my voice slur more than usual. It takes them longer to disentangle the words, to decipher my name, the address, the credit-card number. I sneak small talk in between. How long have you been selling things? Does so-and-so still work there? How come you aren't on a date on a Saturday night? I get my money's worth. The address I provide to mail the paraphernalia is the Salvation Army store down the street.

o

Kal and I exchange small talk. The war crimes trial live from The Hague on TV. Football. Weather. I pretend weather will make a difference to my life in here. Or football for that matter. Kal doesn't like to talk about his life. He thinks my life is emblematic of glamour and success, spends time he doesn't have admiring and dusting the frames on the walls first thing every morning. Saves up to go to Beverly Hills. Would like to help his young daughter more with her school math.

"You will be remembered." He steps back and crosses his arms over his chest, admires my framed life.

I nod. By whom? Who reads Who's Who anyway?

Kal and I do crosswords together. Well, not truly together. He helps out with a word here and there between his ins and outs. Keeps the mind busy between what is and what isn't.

o

My ex-wife lives on the other side of the country. Damn airplanes. Take people so far away. A wave of panic washes over me when I think about distance. I ring the bell. Turn the lights on. I'm shaking.

That's how my mother died.

On Christmas Eve, at the old age home, she asked me to stay on; looking at my watch I told her I must dash out for a live interview on Bloomberg after my CEO of the year award. She whispered for me to stay. Just that once.

"You'll be okay. All these kind people around here will take great care of you."

By the time I returned home from the studio I found a message on my answering machine saying the cancer had taken her. She died with the radio on, listening to my interview.

o

My ex-wife phones me on my birthday. She is reliable that way. She assures me she is trying to find a minute in her schedule to fly up, busy with yoga and the step-grandchildren from her second marriage.

"I told you so. Kids eat up your life, your savings, and then forget you. You are lucky to have grandchildren. They like you better," I tell her.

The secretary at my corporate office rings to say my boy is checking the numbers on a new gas well but he instructed her to wish me a happy birthday. She even sings it to me.

When the echo of her voice dissipates in my head, I hear a chorus of rustling steps washing over the corridor. Then a hush and shush of voices bringing unusual quiet to this wing.

Kal walks in holding a lit-up cake and practising his tenor pitch. He is followed by a procession of nurses, the man in the loose cotton clothes blinking in tempo to the song, the midnight woman hiding under a bedsheet, the big tattoo mamma in her restraints glaring from behind the nurses, and the handful of other residents on my floor who can still walk. Not many. I don't know any of these people and they are everything I have.

They surround my bed and sing.

BREATHLESS

DAY ONE
morning

4 a.m. The gong shatters unresolved dreams. The day begins in the dark.

Silent, drowsy bodies enter and exit shower stalls, stoop over the metal sinks, brush their teeth. In a sweaty mirror, Grace inspects the uneven tuft of hair sprouting from her skull, selects the longest thread, glides her thumb and forefinger down its length. Silk-smooth. When she stopped the treatment, her doctors warned she would not live to see her hair grow back into a ponytail. She counts a dozen strands and smiles. It's a semblance of hair. She weaves the flimsy threads into a tiny braid.

afternoon

The dark blinds Grace as she walks into the Dharma Hall. Her eyes take time to adjust to its womblike dimness where light in subtle waves seeps from the pores of skin and eyes, from under the doors, from cushions. She is touched by an immediate sense of the sacred. Grace experiences this tingle whenever she steps into a sweat lodge, a cathedral, a mosque. Spaces steeped in perpetual, rarefied luminosity return her to the first amniotic dwelling of filtered light. She adjusts her meditation cushion and settles into her refuge of silence.

"Eyes closed. Focus on the edge of the nostrils where the air touches the skin." Grace meditates according to the instructions. Not easy when a vulture perched on her flank tears at her skin, its flintlike beak excavating her guts.

"Pain is just a vibration arising and passing," declares the teacher with his rasping voice.

DAY TWO
morning

The second call of the gong, muffled in the distance of sleep, weaves into Grace's dream. The sunflower she holds changes into a cast iron lid sealing the stew cauldron where a venison head boils. The iron lid rises and falls while the boiling liquid tries to escape. It clanks in a syncopated beat; the reverberating knell travels up her spine.

A jet of light douses the dorm and startles her awake. An elderly Buddha-bellied woman from the bunk across stands by the door leaning on her cane. She clenches her smile and stares at the three dazed bodies pulling away from their bunks.

Who are these people sharing her room? Grace does not know. Not even their names. Just as she wished. The last place she wanted to end up in would be a hospital or a hospice, places far removed from open sky and trees. She sighs, relieved she avoided those factories of death. Yes to bodies humming with health to remind her disintegrating body of the continual song of life and its possibilities. Yet these healthy people are also dying. In the agreed silence she understands them by their gritted jaws, tight and anxious eyes. Their old selves crumble before their eyes. A practice drill for the ultimate farewell. The farewell to loved ones, songbirds, basil leaves, stamp collections, harmoniums, and honeycombs.

At breakfast, Grace eats her porridge with full awareness . . . small bites masticated to infinity. The sweetness of the boiled prunes melts in her mouth and slides down her throat, first filling her toes with life and then, slowly, the rest of her.

afternoon

Countless hours of sitting meditation are the most arduous challenge Grace has yet encountered. Give me another Sagarmāthā to climb anytime, she complains when she is supposed to focus on the nasal gateway of her breath. *I crave movement.* Only a year ago she had imagined Kilimanjaro the last summit to conquer in her quest to bag the highest peak in each continent. Now this climb before her body while balancing a cosmic egg timer on her shoulder has caught her by surprise. No goals therefore no distractions.

"Your mind is growing sharper," the teacher reassures everyone.

One more second and I'll die! Grace tries not to sense time. *Please, please, please . . .* But the torturing tic-tac of the mind continues. *For fucking Buddha's sake start the fucking chant . . .* The ungraspable beak ripping at her flank. Each minute is an hour. Minute after minute, stirring her focus away from the pain, her mind attunes to the subtleties around the room: a rustling blanket, dry swallowing, and then finally, forty feet away, the movement of the teacher's arm, elbow joint crackling, fingers reaching for the tape deck, the wings of a saviour. The growl of a recorded chant begins salvation: *yes, yes, made it, made it.* Grace opens her eyes and seeks the teacher's face for congratulatory approval. Impassive, this bald teacher with a raptor nose gazes at all the students, intoning, "Take rest, take rest, we begin again in five minutes."

The vulture retreats, begrudging.

DAY THREE
morning

I don't want to die, pins and needles, *why me, why now,* sacrum muscles tighten, pain intensifies, *ask the redhead to elope to the Caribbean,* subtle pounding at her wrist, toes vibrating to a xylophone beat of Saturday Night Fever. She is a sleepwalker, awakening late on this path. She smiles. But the day is not over yet. Her mind leaps, thought to thought, baboon-like. A grim wave burns up her right leg, a cool quiver on the lumbar. Tibetan monks in meditation melt snow circles around their lotus bodies; bodhi tree, body and mind, vibration and combustion, Buddha physics before quantum theory.

At last, in this cocoon of silence, she finds herself within reach of peace. Here words are understood obstacles, here the face of the unknown is in all faces, here every face is unknown. She understands why elephants and dogs walk away to die alone, in the balm of quiet solitude. The agony of familiar faces panicking to avert the inexorable march of time, grasping to stop the untimely crumbling of her body, proved an unbearable burden to carry. She sighs. Her body already feels lighter.

evening

Students hurry for the dorms after the evening lecture, exhausted from ten hours of sitting. No one lingers in the Dharma Hall to ask the teacher questions.

Grace steps into the dusk. A waft of wild honey pours over her face . . . a lifetime of happiness dancing under her dull nose. Behind, in the shadows of perception, she detects the scent of pine. Further still, the scent of hay. All under the interminable face of the sky. A white-tailed deer, near the aspen grove, grazes beyond the orange-flagged fence surrounding the camp. Intermittent squirrel-chatter fractures the silence.

Tucked away in the dorms, the other students sleep. The third day is complete. Grace, last again, paces the path, prolongs the inevitable close of day.

An orange-breasted robin has waited for her every day on the path, just before the gentle climb to the dormitories. The bird hops across the ground and perches on a sun-bleached deer skull resting in the yellow grass. Tonight she agrees with the bird: wings are unnecessary this late in the day. The robin tilts its head, nods, curious. Grace scrutinizes the sky, weighs in the happiness of stars, the glimmering eyes of her lover in the outside world waiting for her return. Neither she nor the robin disturb the sounds of night sleep.

DAY FOUR
afternoon

On her plate, under the salad, Grace conceals more roasted potatoes than she needs. The noon meal is the last of the day. There will be no potatoes for those people at the end of the line. Scarcity, desire, excess, hidden under a pile of glossy greens on her plate. Fearful of judgement. Buried in guilt. The plate of food is a mirror of her life. She eats in the far corner away from everyone, pressing each potato chunk down her throat. A hungry mind attempts to convince her belly emptiness must be filled. Her body rebels after successive attempts. Grace ends up on her knees, bowing over the toilet bowl. Heaving.

Returning everything . . . and more.

During the afternoon break she lies on the dry grass, staring at a dark cloud growing out of nothing, spreading over the bruised sky. The next one is angel-white. Comforting. A fierce wind tangles the orange ribbons that dangle on the boundary rope only moments after the Buddha-bellied woman has spread out each ribbon at intervals spaced to perfection. The old hungers of the mind endure, acting out old desires, circular dances. The gong sounds. Students drift into the Dharma Hall. The world waits for stillness.

DAY FIVE
morning

The gong calls.

The elderly Buddha-bellied woman snores, with two other nasal trumpets joining her in a jazz suite. Grace tiptoes out of the room and walks to the Dharma Hall. Layers of cushions grow higher each day under the students' crumpled bodies. Flesh avoids earthly descent, avoids pressure on old aches.

"Watch sensations on the edge of the nostrils, on the upper lip," directs the teacher. Heat and tingling, Grace notices. Immediately, her mind tumbles off that moment of awareness, slides down the repetitive and predictable slope of the past.

"Let's talk about happier things," said her mother, last month when Grace confessed that her health would not improve and asked if her parents imagined anything at all they wanted to do. A trip together somewhere? Say, Mozambique, to revisit the overseas posting when Grace had been a toddler. Or was there anything they wanted to talk about before, you know . . . she left. "Ohh . . . dear. You'll only be gone for a couple of weeks."

Her mother assembled an encouraging smile. "And then you will carry on with the treatments at the clinic. Won't you? Dr. Gibson is very hopeful, you know. They say he's the best."

Well, how could they believe she approached death when she had denied it for so long, shuffling from best doctor to best doctor, from holy place to sacred site. Pilgrimages in the hope of a miracle. She believed, they believed. They helped her believe, she helped them believe.

Packing her loose, comfortable silk pyjamas for the retreat, Grace told her parents she had come to appreciate their frugality. Father switching the lights off after her. Mother washing plastic bags and hanging them to dry on the clothesline. They wasted less, they had more, the world stayed wholesome.

DAY SIX
evening

The robin does not meet her on the evening path tonight. She waits and waits. Irritation spreads through her body, hot and sharp. Anger slings its hot arrows into the sky, the climb slowing down their momentum, then they fall and return, sinking onto her bowed shoulders. Even this small joy taken. A malevolent universe telling her, you are alone, no wings will take you elsewhere but here. It hurts and incenses her, no one else, not like this.

Tonight as she rolls into bed, she finds kindness under her pillow. A planet-shaped orange glowing, its sweetness still within grasp. She brings its skin against her face to perfume her dreams.

DAY SEVEN
morning

"Sweep, sweep, follow the energy flow from the crown of the head to the tip of the toes." The words of the teacher guide the meditation. Even with her eyes closed, the bony, radiant face of the teacher illuminates the room.

Grace experiences herself at infinite depths. A current of energy flows through her body. Although now needing to lean against a wall and support her head with a pillow, she feels energized. Subatomic particles rise and vanish, in and out of existence. Vibrations flow. The process of becoming. A flame rises from a wick, burns for an instant, replaced by a new flame, moment after moment. The flame never disappears. An optical illusion. The misconception of continuous identity.

This morning her mind is dull as the edge of a disintegrating cookie. "Sweep, sweep," the teacher instructs, and Grace tries, removing the crumbs and dustballs hiding under consciousness.

afternoon

The teacher's rasping voice echoes in the silence of the Dharma Hall. "Be aware of every sensation, pleasant or unpleasant. Scan every cell and observe, free from craving or aversion. Craving and aversion are the roots of suffering."

The thought of one day not experiencing the liquid fire in a mug of apple cider spreading through her hand and seeping into her body, or never again wading through the fragrant flood of lilacs in spring, brings a frown to her face.

Inch by inch, scanning her body, she stops at the liver. An absence. Is it of feeling? This is the desert spreading in her flesh, dunes swelling. Her body drying up and vanishing in arid quicksand.

Is the song of the robin filling her ears a mere lost echo inside her head?

DAY EIGHT
morning

On day eight death joins her at the breakfast table. It occupies the seat next to her. The cedar smell exiting its pale lips surprises her. Later, death accompanies her on a walk around the orange-flagged perimeter.

The hand of death brushes against her own, the casual touch of mere acquaintances. The warm touch surprises. She expected a cold imprint. The hand leaves her as she steps through the door of the Dharma Hall.

Grace experiences breath as a pulse that impels her being. A wind that visits and departs. Who knows where it adventures next? Into the hollow of a tree? The lungs of a songbird? What unfolds after she leaves her body matters little. She will join the universal whirl of life. Form is unimportant.

Appearing to read Grace's thoughts, the teacher says, "It is our choice whether to experience the present breath as our friend or our enemy." His heavily accented voice reminiscent of another language underneath, filled with sand, surf, and sunshine.

evening

Grace pauses at the entrance to the Dharma Hall, touched by a waft of wind. Whose expiring breath has just touched her? She extends her hand. The trust between her and death grows.

The vulture is an old companion now. Grace does not ignore its beak, nor does she offer it unwarranted attention. This pain is not suffering. She accepts its presence as a bird accepts a gale, and glides the air currents. She spreads her mind and rides the shifting feelings high in the equanimous flight beside the vulture. Alongside a smile. There is more to her and her life than a vulture. Yet, detachment is not indifference.

DAY NINE
morning

A cane awaits her at the side of her bed when she wakes from a dream of flying without wings alongside butterflies in a field of sunflowers: each sunflower revealing the face of the child she has longed for and imagined having the rest of her life to meet. She is thankful for the cane. The earth has begun to tilt in front of her with each laboured step. All unclimbed summits have now come to meet her.

afternoon

Tightness blocks her neck. Her body vibrates, atoms pulsate. Her mind empties. Not a single thought entertained, *aahhhh ... until now ...* The chanting begins. Has she just sat down, or have endless gongs filled the afternoon?

An odd peace envelops her. As poised as a willow tree spawning roots into the earth, feeling the sway of winds, flexing, yet not toppling. Her days as a floating leaf at the mercy of the prevailing currents are not her sole point of reference. Choosing the moment of death is a gift.

Beyond the orange flags marking the perimeter, face to face with the bleached deer skull, Grace rests her face on the ground. The new green against her cheek cools her skin, new life sprouting through the mantle of dry, pale grass beneath her.

She has worn a restless path beside the roped limits. There the grass is dead. Greener on the other side.

Her mind grows sharp as a blade of grass.

o

The wind sighs, the faintest flap of a wing on her cheek. Her eyes nod at your warm touch on her hand. The sun disappearing over the horizon lingers, waiting, waiting for her last words. A final hot breath of cedar.

A kiss.

THOSE WHO FOLLOW

By the drinking whirl, along the creek, near the rusted four-wheeled monster, I await deer. Two sunsets have come and gone on this gnarled branch of the red-skinned tree that is my hunting perch.

At last, as the moon climbs the treetops, a cautious doe steps to the edge, lowers her head and drinks the cool. I lick my lips, crouch, and prepare to lunge when a downwind beat of hurried steps announces a two-legged in the forest.

I lunge out of tempo, before I am ready. My claws miss the doe's neck and skim her rump. She startles away with a mixture of dread and joy, knows she is wanted but not taken. The gash of claws upon her flank did not scratch out her freedom.

The prey understands the predator's need: flesh. Flesh of prey or flesh of mate.

The two-legged arrives in the meadow. This female is running, but she isn't running away from danger, she isn't running toward her mother. I don't understand two-leggeds. They bring fear to the forest, to every place they walk.

Tonight I'll follow her. I'll follow her body and embed the fear of me in her mind. Then, perhaps she will leave the forest alone. She stole the quiet from the night. The night was my only reprieve. Perhaps this last refuge from the two-legged world is now also lost.

Any time a two-legged snares my sight, the air swells, electric as before a lightning storm. I hear pounding in their chests and smell the stench of fear that clogs their pores; their eyes bounce in their sockets as they flee the woods. I'm often tempted to show my face because then our woods fall quiet for a sliver of time, but only until the less courageous ones invade the trails with their servant wolves and the extended arms of steel that spit off deadly claws to sweep the forest dead. Hunting for my food becomes impossible then.

At the edge of the woods, wrapped in the night, disguised among low salal foliage, I crouch and wait. Patience is my companion. The raccoon I was tracking sprints toward the lit deck on the blue house.

I chew blades of grass to fool my hunger, follow the raccoon's acrobatics on the thick foliage of the grapevines, and I'm startled when the sun bursts inside the bulb above the door and a female exits, a blue towel over her shoulder. At the far end of the cedar slats, she walks down the stairs and, at the back of the wood den, stands under rain spraying from a metal spout. I lie down again. A blink later, a male exits the same door to join her. They splash each other at leisure and their voices touch the four arches of the night. That rain must be hot against the cool evening because a mist surrounds their bodies and climbs the sky, thickening the white on the Belly of the Night. I marvel at two-legged magic, making the sky rain at their command, making rain boil like hot springs. They are dangerous.

The raccoon crawls among the vines, stirs the unbearable scent of sweetness. He weaves through the foliage and the fermenting grapes. The grapes fall. On the cedar slats they resemble raindrops that will not break. On touching wood, the grapes will tear skin and bleed. They will stain the cedar redder. The male and female washing each other and mating with the slowness of forest snails remain unaware of the sound of grapes falling. This deafness is their undoing in the forest.

The two-legged fall into deep sleep on the deck. The raccoon curls on a beam. I step into the clearing before the wooden den, paw after paw, and freeze. The sky is moving. Pink and violet splashes arrive from the land of the cold winds. A few more blinks and the colours change to lime green, a peacock's fanned tail fluttering in the sky. For a moment I forget what I pursue. Instead, I listen to crickets and follow the bright stars twinkling against the shifting background. In face of this display, even the earth shudders, and the trees tremble. These tremors have become more frequent, more intense of late, the earth overloaded as a mare attempting to toss the burden from her back. Only I and the trees and the plants notice this shudder of the earth beneath us. The two-leggeds continue their steady breathing. One day their wood den will be shaken so hard it will crumble, crushing them into the earth in their sleep.

I step onto the deck. The raccoon paces in circles on the grape trellis; he stands on hind legs, sniffs the night, brings the long delicate fingers of both hands together. They touch as though imploring. His eyes turn to the stars. He has lived around the two-legged for too long and has learned to imitate them in the face of danger. The raccoon darts across the main beam and over to the roof of the wood den. A shower of grapes tumbles on the deck. The two-legged stir in their sleep. I stop breathing and watch the male's eyes open and stare at the canopy of leaves. He turns on his side, glimpses me, smiles, rubs his eyes and returns to his dreams of a cougar.

Another hunt failed, and today I will not eat. On the deck, I watch the two bodies until their breathing sinks into their chests. My stupid stomach speaks, tempts me to this easy flesh. I do nothing and it growls, angry. I know the two-legged would become my last dinner. They are vengeful. They bring trouble enough as it is.

BARKING UP THE WRONG TREE

The hounds' barking intensified. Far behind them, Gordon stepped up his pace along the forest trail. Clouds gathered above the canopy and Gordon smelled the approaching downpour. In sharp morning or evening air, the freshest scent aroused the dogs and eased the task of tracking but already the day had shifted on them. Rain meant the end of this chase. It was best to return after the earth had dried and the scent of cat's fur rubbed on brush clung to the leaves. Harry and Donald, his apprentices, dragged their feet behind him, sighing the mute song of their increased boredom. A song of their age.

"Patience is the secret of tracking. You're in the wrong business if you're after quick results. Takes days to track a cat, sometimes weeks."

In a frenzy, the hounds stopped by the stream to bark up a red arbutus tree — their front legs clambering and scarring the smooth trunk, jaws snapping and clacking. Gordon inspected the ground, the criss-crossed tracks of the cougar, a maze of directions in, out, and around the tree and to the creek. He lifted his gaze, noting the territorial cat scratches on the trunk.

"Hmmmm?" Gordon pulled up a fern at his feet and chewed on the rhizome stem that grew beneath the moss, savouring the licorice taste. As a precaution he maintained a fair distance from the tree and the impenetrable, dense canopy above him. With a methodical chewing on the stem, Gordon frowned and twirled the sword fern against the side of his face, the serrated teeth awakening his skin, sharpening his thoughts. This cat, familiar with Gordon's trapping strategy during these last three days, seemed to anticipate the patterns of his mind — imbuing this hunt with an inexplicable thrill. Gordon almost did not want this cat dead. It showed such resolve to survive, it deserved to have its life spared. Gordon shook his head to release the grasp of such an outlandish idea. The island people and those beyond, following the hunting saga in the media, counted on him. His pride as a hunter, his success, were held under closer scrutiny this time. After all, the hunter was the one who brought home the kill, not the stories.

A sharp whistle with the aid of his fingers gathered the dogs. He leashed them and admonished the young hound in training, easily overexcited and swayed by the confluence of scents, which led the others astray. Leashes yanking at his arm, Gordon walked his pack of redbone coonhounds along the creek to where the water emptied into the lake. He followed the shoreline to ensure the cat had not waded parallel to shore, exiting further up. "A massive storm cooking," Donald, the oldest boy, said before he gazed further beyond the canopy and added, "Won't be afternoon tea at the Ritz."

"Take the dogs to my place and pick me up in a couple of hours. The scents will wash out in this coming deluge. No use wasting our time, these dogs won't sniff a trail," Gordon said, tossing the chewed-up fern over his shoulder.

As the trail delivered them to their parked vehicles, a drizzle arrived and before the dogs had been locked into their cages it had already thickened to rain. The dogs, restless from hunger, did not stop barking.

"Are you coming with us?" Harry sniffed the air and plugged his nose. "This skunk cabbage stench is bent on tracking us. Good time for us all to catch a shower, no?" He winked at the other boy.

"I see no skunk cabbage around, boys." Gordon swept the parking lot with a brief glance before he stared at the stark clouds. "This is the best time to chew the facts and think like a forest beast, ain't it? I'm staying put. You can feed the media coyotes parked at the store whatever you like. The more outrageous the better," he laughed, emptying his belly of sarcasm as he tossed the truck keys to Donald, disappearing into the woods, a day pack over one shoulder, his rifle over the other. The rain pressed heavier.

A few paces inside the forest, Gordon stood beneath the first large cedar and leaned on the trunk where it appeared driest. An occasional fat drop bounced off the wide rim of his hat, away from his face. In a way, he resembled a cat. He did not appreciate water or enjoy the wet on his skin. He retrieved his thermos from the pack and poured a stream of coffee into his lid to mull over the events of the day and re-evaluate his hunting strategy.

It wasn't long before he readjusted his location under the tree, sidestepping a new steady trickle that had found his hat. He did not want his head under water, under any circumstance. It was a secret held closed. His father had drowned before his eyes. The fishing boat capsized, father and son without floating vests despite his mother's daily warnings. His father grasped him by the shirt collar and told him in a mixture of water and hiccups to hang on to his shoulder, climb on his back. He did. He held his breath and slid over his father's shoulders before he pulled himself to the exposed hull.

"Quick, Gord. Hang tight, never let go. We never give up, right?"

Too cold for words, he had nodded quickly. For a time he dared not move, clutching the keel. As the current rotated the boat he searched for his father. Not in sight. He called and called. Hours later, according to his mother, they found him still calling in a feeble whisper, and for months after, he still called for his father in his dreams. The rescuers thanked an unusual spring sunshine for keeping the child warm enough, on the brink of life. He did not remember his rescue. In his recurring dreams, his father sank in slow motion, waving languid limbs, pulse by pulse falling to hypothermia in the transparent, gelid waters.

After this experience, he refused to shower. On occasion, he wetted a cloth, held his breath, and wiped himself. That was the extent of the chore. It held his social life to a minimum, exactly how he preferred it. And his dogs appreciated him better smelling like the wild. Rain tensed him up. He wondered why he had not moved to a desert yet, a place without water in sight.

He was still nodding now under the tree, watching the rain. His hand moved along the oiled barrel of the rifle glinting in the low light of the forest, his trigger finger tracing the scratched initials on the comb of the gun. He had carried on with his father's gun and, with luck, this would be the sixtieth cat on its count. Twenty of those under his name. Gordon stared at the notches on the butt of the weapon and imagined the scratch to follow. He smacked his tongue against the roof of his mouth and smiled.

It seemed too soon yet when he recognized the engine of his truck returning. Could time have elapsed that fast? The truck stopped short of the park, around the curve, near the ocean. The truck door slammed. The dogs howled and snarled, throwing themselves against their cages. Red-haired Harry, youngest of the two, arrived out of breath, eyes wide as a barn owl's.

"We spotted the cat on the trail, heading to the beach."

FOREST ARCHITECTURE

The hounds' barks ricochet from tree trunk to tree trunk through the dense salal brush. When I reach the slurred part of the forest, I am tempted to climb a tree, steer myself away from the hounds' reach — yet I know that climbing a tree, an ancient strategy, is no longer wise. These servant wolves don't hunt alone, these are hired killers of a two-legged desire for blood, trained to hate, trap, and maul on behalf of their masters. Later, for their murder, rewarded in fresh venison, venison they didn't have to chase to earn its taste.

Two-legged have forced me to think like prey. Predators are fearsome. In listening to my fear I'm now also fearless, having learned to adapt to the two-legged and their arms firing up death, sinking their detachable claws into our white chests.

I smell the two-legged hatred in the forest air. This hatred is the flower of fear, a hunger that will not be satiated until blood coats their hands. I want to maintain distance between my pursuers, so they will not catch a glimpse of my intentions. By the time my pursuers reach the shore I must be out of sight. I leap onward through forest, aiming for the shoreline from where I will swim to the next island, and the next, to wait a few moons until the hunt for my head subsides. Only then will I return. This island is my home.

I am trapped inside this lean forest and must wait for the night. I leap from tree branch to tree branch, enter the denser woods as the light thins out behind me. The shadows will hide me and the slaves will be entangled by the salal maze on the ground. I close my eyes for a moment on this tree perch and take a rest from watching the comings and goings of the bats and owls.

It's dark and quiet in the forest. I yawn and stretch limbs sore from a day of turmoil. With the tip of my tongue I remove a burr from the web of my toes, clean myself from the sweat of the day, and remember my mother.

While licking our pelts clean, Mother told me we too had once been two-legged and have since shed that thin skin to ascend the tree of creation to reach the web of stars. We now suffer at the hands of the two-legged, who don't see outside themselves. Unawareness of what surrounds these creatures and how they affect the forest signifies a lower form of existence. The more we endure two-legged hate and greed, their blood-shedding ignorance, without responding in kind, the more aware we shall become in our climb to the web of sky. And then soon, very soon we shall turn into immortal stars, that's what she told me.

Of course I have doubts about stories told by mothers. My mother wished me not to suffer, she wanted me to steer far from danger, and she loved me to a depth she did not go in loving herself. I contemplate the world, digest its bones through my eyes, and wonder if stories deliver hope. Perhaps my mother wrapped me in words of hope to help me tolerate the immense body of pain she understood was coming.

My mother was murdered on a tree.

My mother, leaping along the forest ground over deadfall and cacti, hounds set loose on us, the barks chasing our tails. I, dangling from her mouth by the scruff of the neck. With a slap of her paw, a growl through her white flashing teeth, she forced me up a thick and impenetrable tree. I meowed, dug my claws into the bark, resisted the abrupt parting. She nudged me on with her muzzle and growled, "Climb to the other side of the sky, our lives rest on your courage."

She led the slave hounds on a wild chase, scrambling down the rim of the canyon to the valley floor, along the river, where the canopy grew thickest. Down the tangle of canyons, against wind and rain, she criss-crossed their current of scents, slowed the tracking servant wolves. She departed without a chance to lick my ears.

My mother killed four hounds with lightning swipes to their throats before the next six trapped her for five days atop a red-skinned tree. Every two days new servant wolves replaced the hungry sentinels at the foot of the tree, and waited for the hunters to arrive from their campfire. The unreachable gargling of the nearby stream tormented my mother, who licked the smooth branches and leaves for morning dew. She could have jumped to her death and ended her agony. Or fought the slaves. By now she was far too weak. Instead, she spotted me on the rim of the canyon and with her piercing gaze insisted I move, assuring me she would be fine. She had seen me follow her tormentors along the canyon ridge. She was proud of me and her eyes glimmered brighter than the stream below.

Unhurried, the hunters arrived days later, howling and firing their thunder along with their laugher, unsteady on their feet. The red arbutus seeds showered the servant wolves every time they shook the tree with their pathetic attempts to climb the trunk. Hunger and thirst tied my mother's throat. She didn't move or fall when the first bullet seared her fur, pierced her flesh. The hunters riddled her. The impact of each bullet shuddered her body, stained her coat, nudged her from the branch, until she collapsed on a barking hound, breaking his spine and killing the slave at once.

A pair of young two-legged lashed her legs to a pole; she departed the forest with her head hanging low. From the top of the cliff I followed her. The servant wolves bit at her tail as it dragged on the ground. Merciless hounds on short leashes. My mother wore her best smile on her death, a smile that returns in my dreams. I accompanied the march from the ridgetop as they trod the valley bottom. The following day I walked away from the rising sun, as far away as I imagined one could.

Unpractised in hunting and the ways of the forest, I survived on grasshoppers, on dog and cat food set on decks. I avoided older male cougars. I replenished my belly on the occasional stray pet, lamb, or calf until I found my way to strength. Under bright moons and thunder skies, through swamps and snow, I walked and walked until I was no longer a young one and I claimed these islands, claimed a thin forest to guard my own herd of deer.

I growl at the raven swooping above me, cawing at my run along the forest floor as I flee to the nearest ridge. He failed to warn me of hunters entering our forest carrying their arms of fire and setting loose their murderous slaves. The raven is punishing me for not allowing him a peck at the juicy bones of a deer.

The hounds close in. I want their muzzles to taste the heat of my fur suspended in air as they sniff my trail through the brush. I want the vegetation to smell of me and lead them to my trap. Leaping over a fallen cedar my long serpent tail brushes a skunk cabbage. I leave a touch of myself, leading the hounds past my tree where they had hoped to trap me. I am nearly out of breath and allow the hounds to gain ground as I near my last buried deer, intoxicating my haters with the maze of scents accumulated over days.

The wolf scampers away as I run toward the site. She is stealing the bones and thinks I am after her. I take no notice. I have no time to teach her a lesson. Soon I reach the bend of the creek and I purr and chuckle, for I hear the slaves' distant barks now running in circles.

I would be purring were I never again to encounter a two-legged in my forest path, but contact is unavoidable. They live everywhere. I recognize the mixture of awe and terror in their faces. Two-legged grow brave behind their armour of weapons or the wheeled monsters that first blind you and then crush you on impact. Flesh on flesh, eye to eye, their legs tremble. The stench of fear drenches the surrounding air and their eyes fade out.

Deer dictate my movements. Their travels lead me closer and closer to two-legged wooden dens and paths, as deer, losing their forest and ferns, find their temptation in the effortless food available in lawns and gardens.

I seek shelter from this unusual afternoon heat that lifts dust from the two-legged pathways. I find a perch near the stream where the cool lifts from the water and rub my stretched belly on a branch. Empty again today, my stomach growls its anger at me, despite my busy legs, fleeing all day for my life. I avoid visiting my last kill site to check if my food stays safe. Deer rots fast in the bright season. Its odour, thick, hangs from everything in that stretch of forest, a spider web of smells that attracts the hungry and draws the attention of my hunter. This two-legged is most dangerous. It amazes me when other two-legged walk past my kills without tripping on the smell. This two-legged understands my language, recognizes the messages I leave on the ground for the other forest dwellers. My hunter is not easily fooled.

I try to forget that deer I earned with my patience and now cannot eat. Instead, I dream of past hunts and slumber on this tree perch. Strands of sound and smell tricot the forest to a web of lives: squirrel chatter, raven's clack, skunk's spray, everything weaving one into another holding my home together. I sigh.

Death will arrive one day. I accept that equation as one who also delivers death without warning. Swift and from behind, faster than prey can think, swifter than their muscles can twitch. A broken neck on impact and their lives have expired without even a sigh. Their lives become the dream it always was. There is no pain, there is no suffering. Unlike the cornered animals two-legged keep around their dens, frightened of the glint they see arriving in the killer hands, not knowing if that is their last moment.

My kills feed the weave of the forest. The ravens, the vultures, the wolves, the maggots, there is hardly a creature that does not fill a belly from my sweat. Two-legged kill us and do not eat us. They kill for pleasure. They kill for fear. I have peeked inside the wood den of my hunter. He hangs the heads of my people and other forest creatures from his walls. I don't expect my end to vary from that of any other creature. I wish only that my end, when it arrives, finds me with composure, the composure modelled by my mother, that like her I will go down fighting, take a few slaves with me, maybe even a two-legged.

Hungry tonight, the sky rumbles. I thank the skies for their help. The rumble approaches until it sits over my head and shakes the tree. The winds push the branches and whistle their anger. I curl tighter against the trunk to avoid the wet and sink my claws into the tree's skin. The clouds overflow this evening; they fill the earth with green.

The hunters began tracking me after they found the two-legged male at the cliff's bottom. They believe I killed him. No. When I leapt from the rock ledge and down the tree to find the two-legged, a thick red spring bubbled from his mouth. He suffered. I crouched beside him. To my surprise, the male smiled, at peace with my company in his death. I learned to respect this fearless male. I saw my face reflected in his eyes when I smelled and licked the blood coming out of his mouth. He smiled. We lay, eye to eye, as intimate ones lie, his body contorted on the ground, deadfall sprouting from his chest, body impaled by the dead tree.

I placed my mouth over his mouth, I covered his head with my jaws. The male tasted my warm breath and gazed into the darkness of the path. The sound of pain could not exit his mouth, flooded with blood trickling down his lips. His hand moved to my head. Did he caress it? He offered no resistance. I closed and twisted my jaws, and death released him. The chest was now still and fearless. I stayed with the body, waited for the male's flesh to cool down, the blood to thicken, before I drank his blood, took his body into my body.

THE SYMPTOM OF BULLETS

Heads down, Gordon and the two teenage hunters dragged their feet on the trail. Returning exhausted and without cougar, they paused by the creek to quench their thirst. The failure of the mission weighed on their pride. The chase had extended to a frustrated week, and this cat still eluded them. At the beginning of the chase, in front of national TV, the bragging words of the boys had guaranteed islanders and the world this cat would return wearing nine shots in its pelt.

"Why so many?" asked the reporter.

"To ensure it won't return to collect the remainder of its allotted lives — at least not on this planet." Harry wiped the freckles on his forehead and assured the fettered TV anchor.

"I understand you're tracking the cougar that killed your friend, Junjie."

"He was no friend of anybody here, a crazy environmentalist."

"I see."

The reporter moved on to a flustered mother with a newborn in her sling.

Gordon had stood at a distance under a cedar tree watching the newscast circus troops setting up cameras. They interviewed islanders posing in front of the old trading post and catching a background glimpse of the mighty twelve-point elk rack over the door. Now a general store, this old post sold everything from rat poison to green diapers, although truth be told they still made the best salmon rolls west of the Rockies.

The locals wore their best strained faces before the glimmering lenses and the children hid behind their parents' legs, shy and afraid of the sudden kerfuffle stirring their quiet village on the shores of Clytosin Bay.

Gordon understood the fear consuming the islanders. Cougars remained the last creature in this dwindling forest to remind humans it only took the swipe of a paw to reduce them to protein. Mortal and edible, humans did not control their fears, even less their destiny. Cougars reminded people no benevolent god existed and that was a truth not welcomed by many.

A flash of speed, a burst of light, a glimmer of death defined a cougar. "That or lightening, take your pick. The chances of survival after being struck by one or the other are about the same," Gordon had warned Junjie when he told him the forest was his home and he'd rather die at the paws of a predator than crushed to a sardine in a highway collision. "He received his wish," Gordon had told the team of forensic doctors reassembling Junjie's body parts a few hours before the carrion-hungry TV crews had arrived on the island.

Gordon crouched by the creek and wiped the day from his face with the cool, clear liquid. He chewed on a fern stem, watching his hounds lapping at the stream. His nose caught the shift in wind and then, without warning, the hounds sprang up the hill and into the thick underbrush at the base of the stone cliff.

Gordon reached for his rifle to pursue the hounds' trail again. Not as excited, Donald and Harry complied, although exhausted by many false hopes. After a long week of being led by his hounds to a maze of old scents and tracks, Gordon no longer understood what trail burned and what trail froze. The real one could surface anytime, though, with a buzz of luck. Judging by the intensity of the hounds' barks, this could be the winner.

Gordon arrived at the base of the cliff ahead of the boys.

The hounds had circled a wolf, trapping her against the cliff base by closing the flanks. They darted in and out, biting, and her fur erupted in the fight. Outnumbered six to one, she snarled and still held the hounds at bay.

Gordon stared at the dogs and the undersized wolf: the empty hull of her ribs and a ragged light coat torn further by the fight. It had been a rough winter for this creature. He raised his fingers to his mouth to whistle his hounds to his feet, when shots echoed in the forest.

The wolf fell with a yelp. The dogs jumped to her throat.

Gordon whistled them to stop and rushed over to chain them to their leashes, tying these with a ring to a wire cable around a nearby cedar. He turned to freckled Harry a few steps behind him.

"What'd you do that for? Don't you know the difference between a cougar and a wolf?"

"May as well rid the island of another pest, don't you reckon?"

"I give the orders to shoot. Do you read that? This creature wasn't hurting anybody, was she?"

"At least we'll get back with something to show."

"That's the last time you track with me."

"Suits me fine, you don't know up from down anyways. A week on these trails and still empty-handed. Maybe if you stopped broadcasting our presence in the forest with that stupid orange floating vest, we might have a chance to blast that damn cat."

"Or if you stopped talking to trees as if they were people. Your hounds are just as insane, barking up empty trees." This from between Donald's teeth.

Harry swung his rifle over his shoulder and walked away, followed by Donald imitating his swaggering steps.

"Aren't you taking your proud trophy to show the family and the girls?"

They pretended not to hear him and walked on.

Gordon aimed. A bullet splintered the tree bark next to a boy's ear. They froze.

"You're insane." Legs trembling, they turned, and leaned on a tree. They shook their legs to bring their thoughts back in their limbs.

"You haven't seen nothing yet." Gordon spat on the ground and steadied his gaze on them.

With grimaces, the boys returned to the wolf.

"Tie up the creature," Gordon said, standing next to them.

The boys snorted and stepped sideways a little, plugging their noses.

"We'll take down that maple over there instead," Harry said, pointing further to the right of the clearing, moving a few metres away.

While the boys hacked a strong young maple to hold the tied-up, dangling wolf between their shoulders, Gordon examined the surrounding area. He traced cat marks up the tree next to the cliff, smelled the bark, rubbed his chin, put his hands in his pocket. The fight between the wolf and the hounds had turned the soil and jumbled the message board at his feet. Here, Junjie's body had been found half-eaten by the cougar. Failing to read a text that had been scribbled manifold, his eyes climbed the cliff's face. He shook his head. The cat hung out here. He re-examined the fracture on the cliff's face and decided it unfeasible for a cougar hideout.

With the soles of his boots, Gordon scraped the layer of green vegetation and uncovered old bones. "Deer. Bingo." The forest floor was this cat's fridge and he had just uncovered the deli section. The wolf had been scavenging a cat kill, not much luck in it, but for an old, starving wolf better than nothing.

He stood atop the cougar's favourite takeout, judging by the amount of clean bones scattered at the base.

He remembered his father on their first tracking trip saying, "We stare at the truth, then explain to ourselves why that could not be, and then, we follow a wrong trail." Gordon chewed on his father's words. They reminded him to relax his gaze, his mind. This was an optical illusion to see through, like the trick picture these boys had placed in front of him a few days back. "What all can you see?" Their eyes expected him to cut across the obvious, the predictable, and he could not. Maybe that's when he had fallen from the boys' pedestal. Somewhere in this picture showing a thick curtain of rain in the forest a cougar supposedly hid. It was not easy to see the layers of possibilities, in any given situation. It turned out the cougar was the rain itself, disguised in drops of a subtly altered hue. What would be the outrageous questions in need of asking for this cat chase? Perhaps they were chasing two different animal species here. Or two cats? No cat at all? Gordon could see the boys mistrusted his uncertainty, too young to see that it prevented complacency.

As the boys finished defoliating the maple and hacked the last twigs from the pole, Gordon prodded them once more.

"Now you've got yourselves a nice good hike out carrying the wolf on your shoulders, and God willing, maybe it'll also weigh on your conscience so you get some sense into those heads. Anyways you'd better come up with a fine tale for the conservation officers by the time you get into town."

The boys shrugged and they rolled over the wolf's body and kept their mouths shut.

Still probing his uncertainty, Gordon pondered the reported sightings of a white cat. The rare occurrences of white bears and white whales were known to him. But an albino cougar? A wild white cat should not last a season in the wild, the white coat announcing its presence to any hunters with eyes to see. Nature just did not function like attention-seeking tabloid stars. Nature did not want one to stand out, draw attention, become vulnerable. Maybe the pale grey wolf and not a cougar was the elusive predator the islanders claimed they'd seen circling their houses, stealing dog and cat food. Before the boys tied the wolf to the maple he checked its teeth, pressing the tip of his cowboy boot in the mouth and pushing the lips aside. The worn and missing teeth showed her too old to hunt for her keep. With a deluge of cougar sightings and stories on the island, no one saw other possibilities anymore. Even fleeting glimpses of other animals were at once imprinted with the cougar fear. The mind perceived what it was instructed to perceive. He would phone his tracker buddy in Montana that night to tweak his brain and pry open a new window in his mind.

THE MISSION

I weave a maze of scents through the forest. The hounds, excited by the anticipation of blood on their lips, follow endless circles, unable to distinguish the hottest trail. I leap into the shallow creek, avoid mud and puddles, and move down slope with the gurgling water. My whiskers detect the current of air in the forest, a three-dimensional map of everything that stands in the way of the breeze and changes the flow of air. Registering deer nearby, my stomach rumbles. I cannot stop. I've counted six moons since my claws sliced open the belly of a raccoon and my muzzle filled with the warm juice of entrails.

Lungs, spleen, liver, pungent in my mouth. The choicest organs first.

The hunters, desperate, imitate the mating pitch of a female. Two-legged will imitate anything. They are worse than ravens. Had I not known that a female scent isn't present in my range, that tree scratches or urine markers are absent, I would have been tricked in the same way the two-legged trick each other. I hold my breath. A young cougar, only hours on the island, foraging for new territory, crosses the clearing. He sniffs the air, tail twitching, then follows the treacherous song. A gay trot to his death. I tell this young puma nothing and I earn a bad taste in my mouth. He will be the sacrifice that will deflect their attention from me. The two-legged will leave me in peace a while longer, imagining the cat they sought at last snared.

Dusk wraps the sky.

My wide paws absorb the crunch of a leaf. I walk the forest as though the forest bears no voice to denounce me. I walk and walk, with more care than usual, until I first smell the ocean and then I hear the lapping waves.

At the edge of the forest I stop, listen. A guitar strums, wood crackles, a hum of singing arrives at my ears. Beneath the stronger smell of wood burning, the smell of roasting camas root drifts along the shore. The silver claw rises from the ocean and as it travels, opens the belly of the sky, which bleeds the most unusual red. The tip of the claw points to the next island. To protection.

The sky bleeds the last of its blood before the dark entrails of the night appear on the horizon. I cannot wait, and trot along the forest edge, risking tracking by the hounds, seeking the height of boulders to conceal my ocean entry. Crouched low to ground, I crawl toward the ocean as though I stalk a prey, and enter the water, rotating my head for a last assurance my pursuers are not in sight. I swim toward the dark mound of another island in the distance.

BLACKBIRD

On the tips of his toes, the father crossed the lake of splattered figs surrounding the tree. He approached the cage cradled on the lower branches. The son tucked away his duffel bag under the double swinging chair and joined him at the bird cage.

"Father, does the blackbird still sing?"

"Here and there. It's getting into the quiet season anyhow."

The father turned his attention to the bowl of seeds in his hand. With care, he sifted the seeds, ensuring only the very best reached his captive bird.

"Can't trust commercial feeds any longer. In business to swing a buck. No love for the creatures."

Squeezing his hand into the cage, the father nestled the

seed bowl in the far corner against the mesh wire. He changed the bird's water while the son collected a handful of figs from the tree. The bird hopped to the farthest top rung of the cage and observed the son with curiosity.

Together, father and son strolled back to the double swinging chair under the persimmon's foliage and sat admiring the coal-like shine on the blackbird's plumage, his bright orange beak.

"Only birds pluck their feathers to provide offspring with the comfort of a nest!" The father's words hung suspended between them.

The figs, fermenting on the ground, perfumed the air. The son whistled the blackbird's song. The bird responded.

The father smiled.

Father and son listened to the blackbird's fluted warble, perhaps his last melodious canto before he changed to winter plumage and fell silent. It would be weeks before his voice would return with the first hints of spring.

"Has the wing healed now?" the son asked. He parted a ripe fig in half and dug into the flesh with his teeth. Succulent juices dripped from the edge of his lips.

"Oh yes, some time ago now."

Last year, after only hours in the world, the bird had fallen from the nest and broken its wing. The father had rescued him from the base of the persimmon tree and, under a kitchen lamp, he had nurtured Blackie to health, feeding him fresh worms and crushed beetles.

"Maybe now Blackie is ready to return to the skies, father?"

"Can't invite trouble, my son. Such a cruel thing to do. So many cats and ospreys around. Wouldn't last a day in my count."

"What about those? They seem happy." The son pointed to three blackbirds circling them from above.

"Not Blackie, my son. He has never tasted the outside of a cage. It's a dangerous world out there."

The three blackbirds landed on the enclosure's railing. They called to Blackie, who hopped down from his tiny swing and pressed his body to the wire mesh. They rubbed beaks in a greeting. Soon the wild birds departed and returned in shifts, arriving with fresh worms wriggling from their beaks. Back and forth, convoys of aid flew to feed the caged bird.

"They don't trust us to feed their own. Could never tame those used to freedom." The father interrupted his words, his dull eyes wandered the sky. After a long pause he concluded. "Impossible to fit the wild ones into a cage. I've tried. Their wings broken after endless days banging their bodies against the wire. Bone against metal. Blood running from their beaks. They soon die. Their last breath, one last run at the wire and happy to depart. Souls escaping through the tiny holes in the mesh, and again crossing the skies, I suppose."

The son followed the undulating flight of the three blackbirds across the blue. The birds vanished and his gaze returned to the caged bird, which hopped from swing to swing inside the cage, running up and down the miniature ladder, up and down.

"See. Blackie is content," the father said.

"He has just grown used to his cage. It's the best thing in his tamed horizon."

The son whistled. The blackbird did not respond this time.

"Our family carries the love of birds in our veins. Your grandfather raised turtledoves. Smooth and warm as a mother's bosom. The cooing always near and sweet. Can't cuddle them in the skies."

A gust of wind plucked a few leaves from the fig tree. The son wanted to voice something about the changing weather, the changing times, but his father continued.

"It would break my heart to see a family tradition die, son."

The leaves still swirled in mid-air when a second gust lifted and carried them over the rooftop. The son stood up. He reached under the chair, swung the duffel bag over his shoulder and stepped toward the iron gate. At the gate he stopped, turning for a last glance at the silent blackbird. The bird stretched its beak through the mesh wire for a peck at a fig splattered on the branch supporting the cage.

"I'll write," the son called and strolled into the luminous morning, nibbling on the flesh of a ripe fig.

ACKNOWLEDGEMENTS

I wish to thank the British Columbia Arts Council and the Canada Council for the Arts for awarding me grants that enabled me to complete the writing of this manuscript.

I would also like to acknowledge the following Canadian or International editors and their magazines, in which a few of the stories in this book previously appeared: *tsé tsé* (Argentina), *LINQ* (Australia), *southpaw* (Australia), *Gaspereau Review*, *The Toronto Review*, *dANDelion*, *Esquina do Mundo* (Portugal), *Voz do Caima* (Portugal), *The Queen's Quarterly Review* and *The Nashwaak Review*.

My first readers: Heather Steel, Nowick Gray, Lucy Nissen, Jim Prager, Richard Therrien and Galen Bullard.

Barbara Scott for seeing the diamond in the rough and believing. And in these times of dwindling faith in the fine craft of the written word, I am also grateful for the enthusiasm and faith in my work by the entire team at Freehand.

The following stories are dedicated to:

"Breathless" — Avó Maria Teresa, Tia Maria (Vermoim), Joyce Steel, Jane Eames, Katherine Wollenberg, Tom McKay and Misha Butot who have all danced (or are still dancing) with the vulture of cancer. And also to the many unnamed family members who supported them in this journey.

"Hell's Hell" — Agostinho Costa

"The Green and Purple Skin of the World" — Cecelie Kwiat and B.Q.

"Blackbird" — Koah Skye, o seu *Avô A. C. e Bisavô Manuel Costa*

"Those Who Follow" — Diane and Mike McIvor for giving me the first set of green eyes that forever changed the way I saw the forest and her inhabitants

paulo da costa, born in Angola and raised in Portugal, is a writer, editor, and translator living on the West Coast of Canada. paulo's first book of fiction, *The Scent of a Lie,* received the 2003 Commonwealth First Book Prize for the Canada–Caribbean region and The City of Calgary W.O. Mitchell Book Prize. His fiction and poetry have been published in literary magazines around the world and have been translated into Italian, Chinese, Spanish, Serbian, Slovenian, German, and Portuguese.